Two, Two, Lily-White Boys

Two, Two, Lily-White Boys

a novel

Geoffrey Clark

RED HEN PRESS | *Pasadena, CA*

Book design and layout by David Rose

Library of Congress Cataloging-in-Publication Data

Clark, Geoffrey, 1940–
  Two, two, lily-white boys : a novel / Geoffrey Clark.—1st ed.
    p. cm.
  ISBN 978-1-59709-227-2
  I. Title.
  PS3553.L284T86 2012
  813'.54—dc23
                    2012004617

The Los Angeles County Arts Commission, the National Endowment for the Arts, the Los Angeles Department of Cultural Affairs, and the James Irvine Foundation partially support Red Hen Press.

First Edition
Published by Red Hen Press
www.redhen.org

For Pamela

Two, Two, Lily-White Boys

Sometimes I don't know which is better:
The land at the edge of the water
Or the water at the edge of the land.

—Thomas McGrath, "At Lost Lake"

A man needs only to be turned around
once with his eyes shut in this world to be lost.

—Thoreau

One

I stood watching as my mother, Gracious Carstairs, backed our pearl gray '47 Chevy two-door cautiously out of Camp Greavey's parking area, paused, then slowly drove out the wide gravel road by which she'd brought me here. Sunlight flashed on the windshield, then on her silver-blue hair.

She was almost the last to leave, and the car itself looked sort of sad as it wallowed slowly over ruts—Kenny at the Sinclair station in Ermine Falls had advised Gracious she needed new shock absorbers, but she was waiting until school started up in September and she got her first check. She hadn't told me so, but I figured she was using the money she'd've used for shocks to pay for my week here. And she'd even hinted I might have a second week if I was really having a great time.

And then she went around a bend, trailed by a cloud of dust that quickly drifted away, and was gone just like all the other parents.

Just before she'd left she'd hugged me to her saying, "Oh, remember, Lamar, you are my beloved son in whom I am well pleased . . . oh, don't look sad, and do please, *please*, always be careful!" I wasn't very sentimental but still my throat felt swollen and my eyes almost teary.

But then I remembered that here I was, after all, back at Camp G, as we all called it, where I wanted to be.

Around me milled uniformed Scouts who like me had made their goodbyes to parents, brothers, sisters, aunts, uncles, and other well-wishers, a few looking eager and well-adjusted to things, more looking anxious, a few downright scared.

Besides me, there was only one other Scout here from Ermine Falls Troop 52—Andy Dellums, fourteen, my age, and like me a freshman in the coming fall, a kind of pudgy and unathletic kid, but everyone agreed he had talent. Andy and I were about the only kids in the Ermine Falls School that were thought to have some kind of (as Gracious would have said) "artistic bent": I was always trying to write stories, while Andy wanted to be an actor—he sang pretty well, was always on-key, could tap dance, play the piano, do soft shoe, and usually dominated our school plays. Unlike me, he was really pretty good. I hadn't yet spotted him. It was a much smaller group this year, only forty-eight Scouts, including two counselors per pod; last year, my first at Camp G, there'd been over three times that many.

I still wasn't sure why Gracious thought I had looked sad because I really wasn't—though now that she was gone I was finding the lump in my throat her final hug had given me was still at least partly there.

As others kept craning their heads, looking in the direction their departing parents' cars had taken as they waited for whatever was going to happen next, I turned to look at the main building, the dining hall and kitchen complex called the Lodge, before which stood the tall flagpole beneath which a Scout each morning last year played Reveille on a bugle; other bugle calls had been made throughout the day but they were recordings. I was guessing that a Scout bugler would soon play Assembly. Or someone would play a recording of it.

The massive Lodge was made of thick cedar logs, like almost all the structures here at Camp Greavey. I knew pretty much where everything was and pretty much how things operated because I'd been here last summer for two weeks rather than the usual one— I'd had such a good time the first week I'd begged Gracious to let me do the extra week and she did.

If things went really well this week, maybe I'd ask Gracious for an extra week, shocks or not.

It was Sunday, August 16, 1953, and I'd see Gracious next on Wednesday when she came over to watch the evening waterfront games and contests. And then she'd be picking me up at camp Saturday afternoon after we'd all finished marching in the Cherry Festival parade in Traverse City. If I decided I wanted another week, I'd have to ask her Wednesday.

When I turned away from the Lodge, I found myself looking up into the scowling face of Nick Whipple, a guy I'd known, sort of, since my Cub Scout days when I belonged to the pack in Skeegemog, eleven miles east of Ermine Falls—we're about 100 miles south of the Straits of Mackinac.

But why such an ugly, scornful look on his face? Nick was eighteen, an Explorer Eagle Scout, and he tended to look contemptuously down his large blade-like nose at anyone not of his circle of mostly Life and Eagle Scout counselors. He'd always been extremely attentive and courteous to Gracious when she drove me to Skeegemog for pack meetings. Mrs. Arlene Whipple was our Cub Scout Den Mother and his actual mother (she called him Nicky).

I'd always felt a certain admiration for him even though he'd always looked at me with contempt.

Now his sharp almost-black eyes fell on my sash with my five merit badges and at my Star Scout pin on my shirt.

"What Wheaties box you find your badges in?" he asked sourly.

"I earned 'em," I said sullenly, lifting my head, looking him right in the eyes, not blinking—sometimes I made people uncomfortable that way just for the fun of it. I've never been out-stared.

Nick was lean and strong and kind of cruel-looking, and though he laughed and smiled a lot, you could tell it wasn't natural.

Nick sucked in a breath as though he were going to launch into something, but then said softly, conveying his utmost disgust for me, "Shit."

He shifted his gaze, looking beyond me, spat on the ground, then wheeled about and stalked away.

I had to admit his sash with twenty-four merit badges was pretty impressive, not to mention his gleaming Eagle badge.

I looked at the merit badges on my sash: Swimming, Stamp Collecting, Photography, Canoeing, and Scholarship. I was hoping I could complete most or all of the requirements for Lifesaving while I was here this time—and now, like I often did, I got mad after something happened instead of during it: You prick, *Nicky*, I *earned* my goddamn badges fair and square. I worked plenty goddamn hard for'em—and you're only four years older than I am, so who the hell do you think you are?

I felt like giving his retreating back the finger. And looked guiltily around. No one was interested in me.

Just then an announcement rained down on us from various speakers, startling us: "Starting now, Scouts," boomed a mellow baritone, "you all have twenty minutes to find your assigned tent pod and stow your gear. Should you be confused, seek out a counselor. Assembly will sound and we will quickly assemble and come to attention before the flagpole again and I'll take you all on a quick tour of the grounds and facilities. That will take approximately twenty minutes, then shortly thereafter Mess will sound: so step lively and hop to it, lads!" There was a scraping noise and the speakers went dead.

The strong clear voice had clearly been that of the camp director, L. Perkins Gibb, nicknamed "Perky." He was well-named, for it seemed like some secret electricity that most others lacked coursed through him like a river. He was at least six four, maybe more, with long hairy arms and legs that were lean and flat-muscled like an animal's. The hair made his limbs look gigantic. People often speculated about what the L stood for, but nobody knew, as far as I knew anyhow. His hands were large and long-fingered.

I'd gotten a glimpse earlier of Perky entertaining a group of parents, holding their attention utterly, and, just like last year, he was dressed like a Scout but bore no insignia even though he was on a lot of Scout boards and committees. He wore Scout-like khaki shorts and short-sleeved khaki shirt and a Scout-like broad-brimmed hat. And knee socks and well-worn hiking boots. At his throat where a Scout'd have worn his official neckerchief, Perky wore a knotted and ordinary sweat-stained red bandana.

I followed a familiar path about twenty yards into the woods and found my tent, 13B, in one of the six four-tent "pods."

The pods had been created, according to a counselor last year, on the theory that smaller units would "inculcate camaraderie" and a "sense of esprit" and "identity," and pods were encouraged to visit other pods and establish a "rapport" with them.

One of the tents in each pod belonged to two Eagle or Life Scout counselors, generally juniors and seniors in high school, who were supposed to watch over us and advise us.

The heavy canvas Army surplus tents were mounted on wooden platforms about a foot off the ground. I stepped inside 13B, inhaling the army-surplus-store smell of sun-heated military canvas . . . and discovered my apparent tentmate unpacking a duffel bag on one of the two cots . . . except all he'd unpacked so far was a book, which he tossed on his cot face down so I couldn't read the title. He dropped his duffel bag on the floor and kicked it under the cot, then turned to me. He wore a Scout shirt and shorts but had no neckerchief. His pin was First Class. He was lean and wiry and easily three or four inches taller than me and his skin looked like butterscotch—he'd likely spent a lot of time in the sun. Everything about him seemed finely and delicately made: his thin nose with flaring nostrils, his long limbs—even his hands and fingers—covered with fine blond hair, his eyes brown; but what you focused on most was his hair: a dark golden mass of corkscrew blond curls, the kind some girls would kill to have. But what really struck me were his hands, for his fingers were very thin and extremely long.

"I'm Curly," he said, his voice kind of high and fluty, "hiya, there . . ." He put out his hand. His long fingers were cool and smooth and strong.

"Hi. I'm Larry Carstairs . . ."

He did a kind of comedian's double take: "*Larry!* Wow! Hot damn!" His almond-shaped eyes were suddenly backlit with excitement. "Now what we gotta do, see," he said, lowering his voice, becoming a gravel-voiced movie gangster, "de ting is, see, we gots to find us some joik here named *Moe* . . . then we can be The Three Stooges! Wouldn't that be great—maybe we can work up some kinda little thing for skit night!"

"You been here before, huh?"

"Yeah. Two years ago. *Ny-yuck, ny-yuck!* You?"

"Yeah. For two weeks last year."

"Troop 52, where's that?"

"Ermine Falls, 'bout twenty-some miles north of here . . ."

"Think we went through it once going to Mackinac Island."

"Yup. You would, likely."

"Hey, Larry, y'ever hear the one about the queer who's on the phone calling up the Thirty-Second Street Ferry?"

"Don't think so . . ."

"Well, y'see, he calls up and asks, 'Is this the Thirty-Second Street Ferry?' At first he doesn't hear anything, then he hears this nigger voice say, kinda real slow-like: '*Thhpeaking . . .*'"

"I don't get it." I never laughed at jokes I didn't understand.

"The boogie's a *fairy,* Larry! A queer! *Thpeaking,* ya know?"

"Oh."

"Here, try this one on for size: this boogie queer's coming down the street holding hands with a sailor . . . and his pal Rastus hollers out to him, 'Hey, man, whatchoo doin'? You a Catholic so you don't get no meat on Friday.' 'Oh,' says the queer, 'this ain't *meat,* man, this here's *sea*-food!'"

That one I did get, so I laughed a little even if I wasn't crazy about queer jokes. Or nigger jokes. Or even hunkie or polack or greaser jokes. Still, I had to admit, Curly had a pretty nifty delivery and something about him made you want to have a good laugh with him.

"Hey, you look like a good guy, Larry, here, you want this?" He held out his closed fist palm down and like I was hypnotized I stuck out my hand palm up. A large darkish coin fell onto it. I looked at it but couldn't read what it was in the tent's gloom. "What is it?" I asked stupidly.

"A penny! Good as gold! A genuine 1820 U.S. copper penny. It's valuable—I'm a numismatist! Not to mention a philatelist! Among other things!"

"Geeze." I really wanted it, but he was goofy and I knew I shouldn't. "Thanks, but I—"

"No objections! Here! It's yours forever, from me to you! Stick'er in your pocket and don't mention it again. Just be sure you never wash it or polish it, that'd lower its value."

"Umm, okay . . . thanks again." And I did as I was told, figuring as soon as I was alone I'd see if it was what Curly said it was. What the hell kind of a dipshit name was Curly anyhow? And what kind of a guy would give away a coin worth something to a stranger he'd just met?

"My real first name's Russell—Russell Norrys, that's N-o-r-r-y-s, okay, not N-o-r-r-*i*-s? Betcha wonder why I don't go by Russ, or Rusty, or something, huh?"

I wondered if he'd somehow read my mind.

Curly shook his head like a tree in the wind and his curls bounced. "Well, it's because I was just always called Curly as a kid and it just kinda stuck to me."

"Oh."

"Make sense to you, Larry?"

"Sure thing. My real first name's Lamar, but everybody's always called me Larry, except for my mother, sometimes. I'm an only child," I added, wondering why.

Curly looked struck and startled by what I'd said. His eyes were round and moist. He stuck out his long-fingered hand again: "Well, Christ's teeth, so 'm I, that makes us practically blood brothers, Larry!" When he squeezed my hand I was amazed at the strength of his slender fingers.

Personally, I'd never much liked people who were always shaking hands.

"Well, shit," Curly said, "guess I better put this sumbitch on," and he pulled a crumpled Scout neckerchief from his hip pocket and tied it carelessly around his neck with a half-assed square knot. "The show must go on."

When we stepped outside, we saw two guys from the closest other tent, and one was Andy Dellums.

They approached us and Andy stuck out his hand, grinning, obviously glad to see me. Behind them from beneath the flap of the nearest other tent in our pod I could see a small white face peering out at us from beneath a lifted flap.

The flap dropped.

There was no sign of activity at the fourth tent, the one for the two counselors.

"Hiya, Larry . . ." Behind Andy stood a glowering kid in shorts and T-shirt who looked to be sixteen or so, and just standing there he looked dangerous as his eyes roamed about and he shifted restlessly from one foot to another, causing his big calves to flex and bulge. We'd studied body types in science last year, and this kid was clearly a mesomorph, all muscle and sinew and looking like he'd knock your teeth down your throat if he didn't like your looks. Or maybe just for the fun of it. I guessed under the same body type classifications, Andy'd be an ectomorph, and Curly and I'd be endomorphs, sort of. Or maybe Curly was something else altogether.

"Hiya, Andy," and I shook his plump sweating hand, "good to see somebody from home . . . this's my, uh, roommate Curly . . . uhh . . ."

"That's Norrys, there, buddy, Norrys, you forgot already, huh, Larry, Christ, I must not make much of a first impression," Curly said, coming to stand by me, putting his hand out to Andy. I watched as his long thin fingers curled like spider legs around Andy's. I could see he didn't give Andy the kind of hard squeeze he gave me.

"Gooda meetcha, Andy . . ."

"You too . . . uh, Larry and Curly, this's my, um, roommate, Jim Poteet from Petoskey . . ."

"Yuh. Bay View, actually." Poteet put his sinewy hand out to me and his grip almost made me yelp. Then he quickly released me and offered the hand to Curly, whose face was lively with interest. When they shook I saw Poteet's eyes widen slightly in surprise at the strength of Curly's grip.

Then we all stepped back a pace, waiting for somebody to speak again. Behind Andy and Poteet I could see two fairly small white-faced Scouts in full uniform leaving the third tent, but instead of coming over to us they hustled off without acknowledging us, headed in the direction of the Lodge.

"*Moe!* Yikes!" Curly suddenly cried out, turning toward me, "Hey, I think we've found our Moe, Larry!"

Andy didn't know what was going on, but smiled obligingly, eyes alert, trying to pick up on the situation as Poteet's gaze roamed about, looking at everything that wasn't us, a sort of angry look still on his face. For a few seconds his eyes followed the two retreating Scouts from the other tent. "Asswipes," he muttered.

Curly cordially took Andy's hand for the second time, pumping it, saying, "Hey, Larry'n me's thinking about maybe getting up a Three Stooges kind of a thing on Skit Night and you'd be perfect for Moe—you see, I'm Curly, m'real name, and here's Larry, his real name. We'll turn you into Moe, even if it's not your name and even if we don't fit the body types exactly . . ."

I was thinking Andy made a pretty unlikely Moe—Poteet would be more like it.

Poteet himself, aloof, bored, and scornful, was looking up into the trees as if to spy some birds or squirrels.

Just then Assembly sounded. You could tell it was a recording because you could hear the needle scraping a couple of barren grooves before the racket started.

Two

The forty-eight of us, assembled once again into a fairly compact group, seemed kind of small, even paltry—last summer there'd been over a hundred Scouts here, and now some of the company looked about curiously, as though anticipating another contingent would come trudging up.

We stood at a kind of parade rest that Nick Whipple and his roommate, Irwin Kajawski, in their full Explorer uniforms, had marshaled us into. They now sternly and sullenly regarded us, arms folded across their chests.

A squeaky voice piped from the last rank, "Hey, Nick, when we gonna get goin'?"

"Knock it off," Nick growled.

Irwin made a V sign to signify two minutes.

But here came Perky now, advancing suddenly upon us, striding rapidly as always, from the main entrance to the Lodge, long hairy legs gobbling ten yards before I could take a fresh breath.

He faced us like a company commander in a war movie and smartly saluted; we jerkily saluted back.

Nick and Irwin each took a step backward to give Perky the full stage.

"Gentlemen, before we commence, let us salute the colors and recite the Pledge." His voice had a little tremble in it at the end. He lifted his gaze to Old Glory, saluted, and began the Pledge.

We mimicked him. I mouthed the words until I came to the only line I really liked, the last one: "One nation, indivisible, with liberty and justice for all." I liked "indivisible" for the way it sounded and looked and I liked the idea of something that couldn't be separated from the rest or broken into parts by anything.

The Pledge over, now standing at parade rest, Perky addressed us:

"Gentlemen, I must tell you that things are going to be a little different this summer, and, Scouts, since we're smaller in number this season, we propose to take a more laissez-faire approach than usual—we're not about to become Summerhill, um, if you know what I mean; but I do mean that this time, we will as per usual distribute the times for when the various kinds of instruction will be available in various areas, but this time we propose to leave you largely to your own devices and let you make most of your own choices—in this instance, gentlemen, you will be somewhat like water finding its own level. And you can expect a fairly extensive questionnaire to get your responses to the new approach on Friday, or day five—it will I'm sure prove to be of great use in shaping the annual experiences for the Scouts who will follow you . . . but this year we're small enough to be a little experimental . . . change is essential in any organization, great or small.

"There is one area, however, that will be traditionally managed, the waterfront: I will speak to that after we've completed our little tour. And now, gentlemen, saddle up!"

Perky's lanky, rapidly striding form swerves, disappears into a kind of portal in the woods where the tops of high maples meet and are tossed about in light breezes so our bodies are continuously speckled with driblets of bright sun; we scurry breathlessly after him along paths followed by many over the years, but not now particularly worn or showing evidence of much traffic . . . a jog to the left—who can guess whether north, south, east, or west, sign-reading Scouts though we are supposed to be: we can only lurch and straggle in the wake of Perky's great earth-devouring strides . . . some of us are gasping from the strain of trying to keep up with Perky without giving in to outright running.

Our first stop is a clearing about fifty yards into the woods and a squat rectangular building where handicrafts, woodcarving, knot-tying, and camp cooking workshops are held. Cooking pits are nearby, and a charcoal grill made from half an oil drum placed vertically on cast iron legs awaits charcoal and fire.

Perky comes to an abrupt halt, spins around on the heels of his hiking boots to face us as we come to a ragged stop.

"You know, lads," he muses, not winded in the slightest, "I often think the Scouts would do well to create a merit badge in ropework and knot-tying—seems to me a grave omission that we do not . . . a friend of mine, Ed Gentry, a master of knots, will show us some of the possibilities tomorrow evening. I hope you'll all attend. Ed has some extremely useful things to impart to you."

Off again, through the woods to grandmother's house we go again, after a few minutes coming into a cleared area, obviously a rifle range.

"Gentlemen, as you know, there's a merit badge for marksmanship, and Staff Sergeant Julius Exley from Central State University's ROTC Program will be available at posted times. Check the main bulletin board in front of the Lodge. We can accommodate six shooters at one time, and it'll be first come, first served . . . you may apply directly to Sergeant Exley."

Another forty yards or so, another clearing: no mystery here, for there sit the four large targets of the archery range affixed to bales of hay arranged at fifty, forty, and thirty feet, the distances cited in the requirements for the archery merit badge . . . we are informed that Nick Whipple and Irwin Kajawski will be running this show and, we are told, bows and arrows will be dispensed at the handicraft center at 10:15 each morning, for fifteen minutes only.

And sweating mightily, we straggle again after him as he leads us out of the gloomy woods, back to light and the sun's heat, back into the hub of things. Perky's tour for 1953 is almost complete. We assemble again, are addressed by Perky: "Gentlemen, tomorrow you can expect to assemble *en masse* at the waterfront by 9:30 a.m., at which point the two waterfront directors, Bart Hargrave and Bud Harris, who were here last year and so are old hands, will take all your questions and explain to you the process whereby you'll be categorized as Beginners, Intermediates, or Swimmers, and your various limits and areas will be pointed out. There'll be excellent chances to work on merit badges in Canoeing, Rowing, Swimming, and Lifesaving for those so inclined, and at week's end, we will give each of you a signed statement as to how much you have completed by the time you leave on Saturday so you may finish work on the badge back home under the auspices of your own Scoutmasters, Patrols, and Troops . . . now, Scouts, to mess, no need to wait for the bugle call."

Nick and Irwin quickly step forward and Irwin cries out in a reedy voice, "Dis-*missed!*"

In the dining hall I sat with Curly, Andy, Poteet, and the two other guys from our pod, who turned out to be Ned Fangbone (blonde, blue-eyed, and sort of pudgy like Andy), from Alpena, and Steve Crawley (rail-thin, sallow, black-haired, a gaze that turned downward should your eyes meet his), from Bellaire.

The picnic-style tables could each accommodate a dozen, and so the six of us all sat fairly well apart from one another. I'd gone through the cafeteria-style line and been almost nauseous from the way kids piled their plates high and wide: huge gobs of potato salad, spreading piles of baked beans, hot dogs, and/or hamburgers. I had a single hot dog and bun and some potato salad and a slice of bread and a pat of butter. The milk was plentiful and you could refill your glass at the machine at will.

Our table was near the head of the room, thus close to the table Perky always sat at with various guests. This day his two pretty teenage brunette daughters were here, as well as a dignified-looking Scoutmaster from Bay City in the south-central part of the state who was an expert on identifying Michigan fauna—he had a long face and thoughtful eyes, and Perky was almost deferential to him as they talked, leaving the girls and the Scoutmaster's wife pretty much out of things. She was blonde, and kept looking up into the vaulted ceiling as though she expected it to collapse.

Then Perky arose, tapped his water glass with his fork, and all conversation at tables stopped. Silence rang in my ears until Perky spoke: "Gentlemen, we are privileged to have with us today an expert on the abundant flora of this lovely area of Michigan, Carleton James, from Mount Haven, a professor in the botany department there . . . Dr. James, Carleton, would you like to greet our Scouts?"

Dr. James arose. Perky sat down and smiled at his two daughters, who looked more grown up than last year—they looked to be around thirteen.

Standing there at ease, obviously used to speaking to groups, Professor James paused to draw in a breath. Then those of us at our table were close enough to distinctly hear *Puh-futt!*

My heart almost stopped: the guy had performed every schoolkid's secret fear: blowing a fart in public.

At Perky's table, his daughters, Pam and Priscilla, tried to strangle their giggles when Dr. James' gentle eyes fell upon them. His wife swallowed and cast her eyes up at the ceiling, then seemed to be blowing upward at a sticky lock of blonde hair. There were a few long seconds of pure silence. Then Professor James scratched his head.

"Pardon me," he said mildly, "must have been something I ate." And slid smoothly into yakking about the varieties of flora to be found on the various trails radiating out from Camp G—fifteen kinds of trees and shrubs needed to be identified for the forestry merit badge . . . also, he noted, he was a birder and could offer assistance to any wanting to complete the bird study merit badge before he left tomorrow afternoon . . .

As we filed out of the Lodge, Curly had a suggestion:

"C'mon over here, Larry, wanna check out the maggot pits? They're around back."

I'd been thinking about the guy who got away with blowing a fart at mess, trying to figure out if I admired him. I guessed I did. Now I turned to Curly: "Maggot pits! What're you talking about . . ."

"This way. It's kinda neat how they take care of garbage this year, you'll love it—y'know, last year they had this system where they had these enzymes kinda crap that ate up most of the garbage—but this year, a guy who works in the kitchen told me, they use maggots . . ."

"Maggots? You see'em yet yourself?" I was a bit skeptical. And at that moment I decided that yes, I did admire Dr. James the Scoutmaster after all.

"Not yet, but look, there comes my pal right now . . ."

A red-headed college-age guy with a short crew cut like mine appeared from the rear of the Lodge, lugging a half-full garbage can toward an elevated area behind the kitchen where three things that looked like ship's hatches in the movies protruded from the ground. His white T-shirt was sweated through.

"Hiya, Jerry!" Curly sang out.

Jerry looked over and gave us a friendly smile. "Hey, there, Curly my man, how's she goin'?"

"Oh, can't complain, I guess. Hey, Jerry, this's my pal Larry Carstairs, Larry, this's my friend Jerry Bronson. Say, how's about giving us a look inside when you dump that, Jerry?"

"Sure thing." He muscled the can up to one of the ports.

Curly got up close as Jerry seized the iron handle and lifted the first three-foot-in-diameter hatch and carefully pushed it back so the complete hole was available.

"C'mere, Larry," Curly said, "get close up and get a good look."

I stepped up and looked down into the hole: it was acrawl with a dully shimmering and writhing white mass. I stepped back as Jerry got the can up to the portal and tipped in a sloppy mess of watermelon rinds, corncobs, bits of hot dogs and buns, salad junk, slaw, and half-eaten cookies. A few paper napkins floated like flowers atop the horrible stew.

As we watched, the garbage overspread the sea of maggots like an oil slick, then began to thin out and began to slowly melt into the mass.

"What'd happen to ya if ya stuck your arm down in there?" Curly asked, but the way he said it let me know it was for my benefit, that he already knew.

"Nothing much," Jerry said. "You'd just get a slimy arm and hand, they don't eat live stuff . . . you put an arm from a corpse in and after a while they'd strip it down to just plain bone . . . eventually they'd even take care of a horse, but it'd be a slow process . . . throw in a dead squirrel in on top of 'em and it'll take, say, maybe a day before it completely disappears. 'Course if all the grub stops and they got no place to go, then I s'pose they'd eat each other until I guess there'd be just one left . . ."

"Wow," Curly said. "The Conqueror Worm. Pure Darwin, just like us."

"Yeah, that's really kinda neat," I said, wondering what it would feel like if I thrust my arm into the center of the writhing mass.

When Curly headed back to the pod, I went toward the waterfront though I hadn't seen any activity there earlier. As I walked toward it, Lake Greavey gleaming like glass before me, the two lifeguard towers looked for the moment abandoned. The entrance was through an open gate on a chain-link fence—all who entered the waterfront were to pass at that point and no other.

Last year I'd bunked most of the other stuff and spent almost all my time on the waterfront. I was fortunate to get away with it. For some reason, older guys often took a shine to me, though Bart and Bud last year often ribbed me about my youth and inexperience, at first referring to me as "Greenhorn"; but they never ran me off and seemed to enjoy my presence. Maybe it was because they wanted to teach me something. Anyhow, Bart and Bud had made a kind of pet of me last year and after they found me useful, they made a kind of project out of refining my style in breaststroke, sidestroke, and crawl.

Back in the tent, Curly's back was to me when I entered.

"Christ's teeth, Larry, I hear they're having their goddamn 'song-fest' tonight, Christ I hate that word—you gotta stay for that crap in the Lodge after dinner?" Curly asked over his shoulder.

"I dunno . . . probably not much else to do."

"You might be surprised." Curly suddenly turned toward me, his long thin uncircumcised cock hanging down from his fly like an exhausted snake. He reached deep into the left pocket of his shorts and pulled it inside-out and let it hang down.

"Take a look at this, Larry. Know what that is, it's my imitation of a one-eared elephant."

"Oh yeah . . . see whatcha mean . . ." But I knew something like disgust must have spread itself across my face before I could stop it.

But that only delighted Curly: "Hey, you're okay, Larry. Sorry if I scared you . . . but I didn't think you were one—that's just a trick I sometimes use to tell . . ."

"Use to tell what?"

"No, for Chrissake don't look at me like that, Larry, it was just my little test, you see—and no, I'm not a queer, Larry, but I'm a queer-*spotter*, God, I hate queers . . . and when I do the one-eared elephant, you see, and a guy's eyes light up and fasten onto my dick, well, I generally can tell right away . . . and I may figure some way to fix his ass, probably not right away, but I'd kinda wait for the right moment and then, well, fix 'im . . ."

"Like how?"

"Glad you asked." But he didn't answer, looked down at his feet which were long and narrow, then asked: "Ya gotta girlfriend, Larry?"

"I . . . well, maybe kinda . . . but not exactly . . ."

"She gonna be coming over for Waterfront Night?"

"Well, uh, no . . ." It occurred to me Alex Fuller might after all follow through on his promise and come over with Gracious so maybe there was a possibility his sister Deanna might come too on Wednesday afternoon for the evening aquatic games. Deanna was my age, yet I couldn't call her my girlfriend, though on our last day of school in May I'd almost reached out and taken her hand when we walked home from school together.

For dinner we had Swiss steak, mashed potatoes, succotash, salad, chocolate pudding, ice cream. The place seemed even more cavernous than it had at lunch. Our voices seemed puny and lost somewhere in the huge dark vault above us, but that didn't seem to bring us physically closer, for each pod-group continued to use a dozen-person table so we could each have an empty seat on either side, with the exception of Curly and Andy, who for no reason at all sat side by side.

This time we didn't just saunter out when were done. An Eagle Scout—in our case it was Nick Whipple again, who let us know he and Irwin were going to be the counselors for our pod—at each table kept us there: we were going to have a "songfest," Perky had said earlier. And now he rose from his chair: "To aid our digestion after dinner, Scouts, we shall now lift our voices to the rafters!

"I'll start us off with an old favorite; if it's unfamiliar to some, try to sing along once you get the repeated verses down. This one has plenty of repetition: O, I'll sing you one-O, green grow the rushes-O, what is your one-O?

> "*One is one and all alone,*
> *And ever more shall be so . . .*
> *I'll sing you two-O,*
> *Green grow the rushes-O,*
> *What is your two-O?*
> *Two, two, lily-white boys,*
> *Clothe them all in green-O . . ."*

A little later, Perky led us forward in his wonderful on-key baritone into a rollicking version of "Down by the Station (Early in the Morning)": "See the little puffer-bellies all in a row," we sang as loudly as possible, but not nearly loud enough to make much of a dent in the cavernous and gloomy interior of the Lodge, Perky's voice guiding us and keeping us more or less together: "See the engine driver pull a little handle: *Chug! Chug! Toot! Toot!* Off we go!"

And so it went, me finally just half-mouthing the words as one song followed another, informing the air that you are my sunshine, my only sunshine, and don't sit under that apple tree with anyone else but me, and shine on, shine on harvest moon, and someone's in the kitchen with Dinah, strumming on the ole banjo, and you are gone and lost forever, oh my darling Clementine.

But now, I've reached my limit. All this noisy good cheer is starting to drive me nuts.

I push my chair back, get up, sidle along the wall trying to be inconspicuous, and whisk outside, trailed by voices piping "Green Grow the Rushes": "Two, two, lily-white boys, clothe them all in green-O, One is one and all alone, and ever more shall be so . . ."

Before I'm completely out of earshot I hear them start something we'd had to sing in seventh grade:

> "Oh Columbia! the gem of the ocean,
> The home of the brave and the free,
> The shrine of each patriot's devotion,
> A world offers homage to thee . . ."

I stop, listen to some more:

> "Thy banners make tyranny tremble
> When borne by the red white and blue . . ."

Then I pick up the pace, eager to be away.

I retraced part of Perky's tour until I came to the archery range, where I sat on a stump by one of the archery targets, its black and white face awaiting piercing by tomorrow's arrows, and visualized my room at home: the plaster plaque titled "PALS," where a cherubic child sits on a stone bench, one arm around the left front leg of a lanky hound; the Bambi and Thumper prints whose outlines used to glow in the dark (I used to think of them absorbing the light of day, then yielding it up slowly back to the night); my two orange crates filled with comics; my brick-and-board bookcases with my Thornton Burgess and other books; my pile of *The Open Road For*

Boys atop my dresser, from which perch my eyeless teddy bear from childhood looks down on things.

Jesus Christ, I thought, I been here just a few hours and I'm goddamn homesick, maybe even bored—I gotta get over this.

I felt better for admitting it to myself.

Then I imagined myself lying in my bunk at home and hearing in the night all the way from Silver Bridge three miles away the snarling engines as outboard racers with their tiny competition marine plywood boats powered mostly by souped-up Mercury Lightning engines held informal races, illegally testing their boats under cover of night.

On a weathered picnic table in our backyard, a whippoorwill often pierces the night with his clear repetitious (and to Gracious, annoying) calls.

Back at the pod everyone was there except me. Curly was seated on a block of wood outside our tent, trying to read a book in the failing light.

The tent Nick and Irving would occupy was still empty.

It was certainly okay with me, but I thought the bastards were supposed to be looking out for us. Steve Crawley and Ned Fangbone were apparently in—I could see an occasional flashlight beam shooting through their flap and falling on the ground.

Poteet had just lit a small campfire he'd built before his and Andy's tent, carefully making a little teepee of wood he'd cut from dead branches with the staghorn-handled hunting knife he wore attached to his khaki Scout belt.

As I moved toward Curly so I could see what he was reading, he called over to Poteet, "Hey, Jim, whatcha doin'?"

"What's it look like?"

"Well, sure suits me . . . it's just that there's this regulation they have here against us doing stuff like that unsupervised."

"Why, you gonna tip'em off?"

"Not me," Curly said easily. "How 'bout you, Larry?" He looked up at me just as I came up to him and I looked down to read the title on the book he'd put open and face down on the ground: *Madame Bovary*. "You gonna tip'em off?"

"Nope, not me neither."

Andy poked his head out of his and Poteet's tent.

"Andy," Poteet said with a mock scowl, "You gonna tip'em off?"

Andy smiled widely. "Sure thing," he said, delighted to be included. Poteet grinned. He seemed to like Andy.

The fire was just about right for the four of us—Fangbone and Crawley had left shortly after the fire began crackling—and as we sat in a semicircle on the east-facing side to keep the smoke away, Andy began to sing "Swing Low, Sweet Chariot." His voice was melodious and true, almost a tenor, and though I felt no urge to join in, I was carried along by Andy's clear voice so that I almost imagined I was sitting in the Church of Christ in Ermine Falls, listening to the choir, led by Gracious, her lyric soprano lofting high above the other voices, asserting itself: "*I looked over Jordan and what did I see, coming for to carry me home . . .*"

But when no one joined in, Andy's voice trailed off mournfully.

"Hey!" Curly cried, shaking his head so his curls danced, "Nuffa this old lady shit—anybody know this one:

"Oh, I grabbed'er by the snatch
an' I flung'er on the grass
and I showed her the wobble
of a—hunnh-hunnh—cowboy's ass . . .

"Y'all know the words to that one?"

No one did.

"Well, shit. Y'*must* know 'Roll Me Over in the Clover' . . ."

We did. Poteet's small fire was doing nicely, just about right for us to be able to see each other.

We had reached "this is number five and my hand is on her thigh" when Perky emerged from the gloom like some kind of spook of the woods. The earlier look of keen energy was gone and he looked like a lot of other exhausted-looking middle-aged men at mid-evening. "Boys," he began, his voice raspy, "lads, gentlemen, Scouts: unsupervised fires are *not* allowed. Douse this one, but immediately. And make damn sure it's good and out. And knock off that filthy singing and go to bed . . . it's been a long day for some of us . . ."

I think at least some of our shock at Perky's arrival was due to his haggard look, the darkish pouches under his eyes, and the roughness of his voice, as if it was costing him a lot not to cough or puke or something.

Back in the tent, Curly was already on his cot, rustling around in a blue nylon sleeping bag almost the color of my own.

I unrolled my sleeping bag, undressed to Fruit of the Looms, stuffed my socks in my tennis shoes and put my clothes on top of my duffel bag, which I kept close to the cot: I sighed, tired, eager for sleep, wanting to be rested for tomorrow, and in skivvies and T-shirt I writhed around a bit in the slippery interior of the bag to get comfortable. I sighed again, this time loud enough that Curly heard me.

"Ya mind if I join ya, Larry?"

"Huh?"

"I can't keep from thinking about fucking this Filipino maid we once had . . . gotta get some new faces'n asses and tits for my 'magination to work with, if you know what I mean . . ."

"What're you talking about?" I was beginning to wish I'd never laid eyes on Curly.

"Oh, you know, pullin' your pork . . . pounding your pud . . . choking your chicken . . . spankin' your monkey, whackin' off . . . but nothin' so rude'n crude as beating your meat, natch . . . it's whatcha gotta do if ya don't wanta get just Christawful headaches, don'tcha know . . ." And he laughed heartily. "Ach du lieber, der bed I haff geshitten!"

I thought again of my empty room in Ermine Falls, the "Sun-room," as my mother and father had designated my west-facing small bedroom, well before Delbert Carstairs died on Omaha Beach near the end of the war. There was something horribly wrong about dying on a beach: beaches were the best places I knew.

"Fruits," Curly muttered into the darkness.

After that I heard nothing further from him, not a murmur, a sigh nor any sound at all as his form seemed to rise and fall within his sleeping bag as he adjusted himself for sleep.

But just as I was drifting off, Curly started up again: "Hey, you heard this one, Larry? Listen, the Norse god Thor comes back to earth for something or other, never mind what, and ends up in Central Park. Well, along comes this gorgeous babe, and without another word they go off to her apartment, Larry, where they just fuck each other's socks off all night long. Well, 'long comes rosy-fingered dawn and Thor realizes he hasn't even told her who he is, so he says to her, 'I'm *Thor!*' '*Really?*' she says. 'Well, me too: I'm tho thore I can't pith!'"

Laughter boils up out of me, poisonous, like puke or a pot going haywire on the stove, and pretty soon Curly and I are laughing our asses off together so hard we're almost crying. After a time, we both run down. Now I'm really exhausted. Neither of us says anything and I can already feel myself falling asleep. Maybe I understand Curly better than I thought. After all, we're both only children.

Three

I woke half an hour before Reveille and quickly got into jeans and a Camp G sweatshirt from last year.

There wasn't a sound of any kind coming from Curly in his sleeping bag and I could see no movement from his breathing. Well, if he was dead, I'd prefer to find out about it later rather than sooner.

It felt good to walk slowly and alone down toward the waterfront on my bare feet, and as I walked I thought about how much I liked swimming, craving it in summer as some did cigarettes. Though I'd been praised for my form, I really wasn't much of a competitor and doubted compliments for something that didn't cost any real effort and was, really, entirely fun. Swimming had always seemed to me something as natural as riding a bike or throwing a softball. Yet there were people—and probably some among the kids here too—who were afraid of water, and who couldn't seem to get the hang of swimming no matter what. But how could you not know how to swim? You just lie down in the water and work your arms and legs in a way that makes sense!

I think I feel safer in or on water than I do in air. My ideal day would be one spent on a nice lake like, say, Silverfish Lake just three miles from my home in Ermine Falls: blue water, sandy shores, hot sun, that great feeling when you first enter the water, the fun of coming out and being warmed by the sun, the feel of drying sand on your skin. Water felt to me the way Gracious once told me cashmere felt to her: "Smooth, very smooth and luxurious, silken, just the loveliest texture in the world, Lamar . . ." In fact, water's the only place I ever feel really free: hell, you can even fly in water, using your arms for wings . . . and you can twist and turn and writhe up, down, and sideways, and just do any damn goofy thing you feel like doing.

I've never felt even a twinge of fear in or on water, not even before I could swim, which I'd easily learned on my own when I was four.

The sun had risen and floated orange and coarse and huge just above the eastern horizon; it looked to be a good hot day, the kind that would be good to spend on the waterfront.

As I approached the entrance gate to the waterfront, I glanced left—and there, coming out of the staff toilet and shower building, came Bart Hargrave and his pal and fellow lifeguard Harold "Bud" Harris.

Both wore terry robes and rubber shower shoes and were walking from the toilet-shower building toward the staff complex of four tents like ours, except theirs were arranged so their front flaps all faced inward, surrounding a little patch of common ground like a tiny courtyard.

I hesitated. Should I step out and greet them, or wait until after breakfast when I'd planned to go to the waterfront? Without meaning to, I took a few steps forward, heading in their direction, then stopped and stepped behind a medium-sized maple—I took a guess Bart and Bud probably weren't very eager to run into any kids at the moment.

"God," I heard Bud say as they passed no more than six feet from me, "this place is looking more like the fucking end of the earth than ever."

"Hey, you're crazy, man, why this here's a reg'lar paradise, sun and water, simple shit to do . . ."

"Yeah, if it just wasn't for the goddamn kids, and if our girlfriends could stay with us, now *that*'d be paradise. Well, hell, leastways there's a real small crew this year, oughta make it a whole lot easier for us."

"No shit, Sherlock."

"But hey, we'll have to look busy or Perky'll have us out scrounging around and policing up the grounds."

"Right you are, pal."

Just then I heard a scratchy Reveille begin on the speakers by the Lodge.

"Well, damn, Larry," Curly said, disappointment in his voice, 'Y'know I was really counting on you coming along today—you look like a real good hiker, and 'sides I don't wanta be stuck all that time with those two goddamn goofs Poteet and Andy, and then to top it off our guide is that idiot jerkoff Nick, whatta prick *that* guy is . . . no, why'n'cha forget the swimming crap, c'mon along, I could really use the company . . ."

We stood in front of our tent. Curly was in shorts and T-shirt and wool socks. A pair of hiking boots were just behind him by the tent's front flap.

"Well, I probably would, but I'm expecting Bart'll want me to help out today with classifying the swimmers . . ."

"Yeah, but hell, that'll be all done by ten or so, right, and right after we're done getting our classifications we'll be stepping off . . . probably the whole balla wax'll include fucking around and getting ready and then hiking'll take us around three, maybe four hours, so we could be back in early afternoon . . . three thirty, four, depends . . ."

"Yeah, but Bart may want me to demonstrate sidestroke and breaststroke dry for them's wanta move from Intermediate to Swimmer in a day or two . . . there's prob'ly six or eight . . ."

"I see you got a real hard-on for the waterfront."

"Yeah," I said, feeling a pull toward saying something like Yeah, so what? What did he need me for? I wasn't sure I really much liked Curly, though he was sure, as Gracious would have said, a live wire. But there was something I couldn't put my finger on that was creepy about him. Yet, he already seemed to know the names of most of the Scouts, and you could see eyes light up when they saw him coming. And he had a good strong laugh. And some of his jokes, about every third one, were really funny.

"Well . . . okay, but it's your ass if Andy falls on top of me and squashes me like a bug . . . or like a maggot ground under somebody's heel . . ." He laughed cheerfully and I felt an inner tremor at the thought of being unable to move while I was covered and consumed by maggots, no nevermind they weren't supposed to be able to eat living flesh.

I decided not to bother with breakfast, so by 8:45 or so I was again walking toward the waterfront, filled with fear that Bart would have to struggle to remember me and that Bud would yawn and not even bother to try.

There it was before me: I wished I had Gracious's 8mm Kodak movie camera so I could do what she called a "pan shot," going from left to right, recording the shore and Lake Greavey, the docks and towers and swimming areas defined by ropes floated by bobbing buoys: acres of lake with the early morning sun glinting off the breeze-corrugated water, trees fringing the lake everywhere there weren't cottages or access points to the water.

Someone touched my shoulder from behind, and I turned, for some reason expecting Curly, but it was Bart, grinning widely, Bud just behind him: "Larry! Old buddy! I was beginning to think you hadn't followed through and come back like you said you would last year—great to see you again, pal, and in fact we could use a little help this morning for separating the goats from the sheep . . . unless you got other plans . . ."

I could barely manage a weak "Bart . . . Bud."

Bart pulled me to him, gave me a quick rough hug, then released me and stepped back to regard me: "So whatcha been up to, sport?"

Bud stuck out his hand. "Yeah, Larry, what?"

"Oh, you know . . . the usual . . ."

Bart winked at Bud: "We'll have to give 'im the third-degree a little later when we got some time."

"Yeah," Bud said, and gave me a wink.

The classification process was done pretty much as last year: Bud sat atop the west lifeguard tower about fifty feet from the main dock, keeping an eye on a canoeing expedition getting ready to set off. He was also to keep an eye roving over the whole waterfront; one lifeguard must always be on duty in either the east or west tower from nine to four.

Bart called the two dozen or so Scouts waiting to be evaluated up to the dock, Andy, Curly, and Poteet among them. I wondered where Fangbone and Crawley were, not that I gave much of a rat's ass.

Bart had swimmers enter the water and swim about fifty feet down to dock's dogleg, where I stood with a roster on a clipboard. Bart called out a Scout's name, pointed to where he should enter the water, then walked slowly along the dock, watching the swimmer until he reached the dogleg, then turned and walked alongside the swimmer on the way back, after which he'd call the name out to me, then "Swimmer," "Intermediate," or "Beginner"—and I'd check off the proper category on the roster.

After evaluation, each time a Scout came to swim, whether for instruction or free swimming hours in the afternoon, he had to hang his round tag specifying his status on a hook on a board at the dock entrance colored-side out, then turn it around on the board before he left.

(Last year when I'd been evaluated thus I'd assumed I'd be an Intermediate and hadn't heard how Bart had classified me, but when Bud handed me my cardboard disk, the top half-moon inside the circle was red with Magic Marker, the bottom half-moon black, and my name in the white middle: I was a Swimmer, the only one from the Troop 52 contingent of eight.)

"Damn, Larry, you look like you put about an inch on," Bart said, checking me up and down.

"Three-quarters, actually."

Despite what I'd eavesdropped on earlier, they both seemed truly glad to see me, and I was pleased Bart remembered me well enough to comment on my height. And I didn't believe it was just because he knew I'd be happy to be a step-and-fetch-it for them again; and it felt good to know I could actually be of some use to them. I'd noticed that older guys often seemed to take a shine to me, mostly, I supposed, because they saw me as someone who needed to be taught something, some specialty which they knew, and if I had any occupation apart from being a schoolkid about to go into his freshman year in the fall, it was being a student of just about anything I found interesting. "My, people sure do like to bend your ear a lot, Lamar," Gracious once remarked. "You know, you're a wonderful listener, and that's really a kind of art. Of course with me for your mother, I guess you *have* to be a good listener . . . or pretend to be . . . I do have to remember *sometimes* to let you get a word in edgewise, as they say . . ."

I stood with clipboard and pen ready. Bart called the next name down to me, "Russell Norrys," and I located Curly on the roster.

Curly obediently jumped in and leisurely sidestroked half the way toward me, then slid smoothly into a breaststroke.

I marked him Swimmer before he finished: I could tell he was a far more graceful swimmer than I with his long, thin but muscular limbs synchronized and moving easily, arms sweeping the water beneath him, his flutter kick smooth, propelling himself forward with never a bit of wasted effort—he was supple as a weasel, or a man made out of eels. He was shivering slightly and his lips looked a little blue when he came out of the water quickly seeking his towel.

"Very nice," I heard Bart say, just before he glanced down at me and called: "Swimmer."

Curly was still shivering on the dock, wrapping himself in his towel, lips still a little bluish. "God," he said out of the corner of his mouth, starting to shiver more violently, "betcha watching Andy swimming is gonna be like watching a monkey tryinna fuck a football. Think I'll slip it. Seeya later."

And Andy was third after Curly, as usual looking around in his characteristic state of wide-eyed, continuous wonder, drinking in everything, as if whatever he was seeing he was seeing was for either the first or last time, his bright blue eyes roving, alighting, moving, alighting again.

Instead of jumping into the water, he sat on the dock, put his feet gingerly into the water, took a deep breath, then pushed himself off, entering feet-first. Once in the water, he labored and splashed his way alongside the dock, doing a clumsy overhand stroke . . . it took him a while to get down to the dogleg.

I'd marked Andy Beginner before Bart confirmed it.

In about half an hour, we were down to the last swimmer, James Poteet, who made a showy arching dive into the water, surfaced squirting streams of water from his mouth, and began swimming toward me.

He was a strong if crude swimmer, and I'd have made Poteet a Swimmer—but there was something about him or his swimming Bart didn't like, powerful mesomorph or not: "Intermediate," Bart told me firmly. Poteet grimaced in surprise. Andy too goggled in wonder that Poteet hadn't made the top grade. It was clear he admired his tentmate.

Our table was completely deserted at lunch, and though I could have moved to a table with some people at it, for some reason it pleased me to be the only Scout at the table our pod favored. Most of the other tables were lightly populated anyway—only about half the Scouts were here—apparently the ten-mile-hike opportunity had drawn some others, who'd have gotten a bagged lunch after breakfast. I wondered how Curly and Andy were going, and especially if Curly were needling Andy because he thought he might be queer.

Back at the waterfront Bart was manning the near tower and Bud was giving canoe instruction by the shore, so I helped out a little, walking down the line of eight Scouts who were dry-paddling according to Bud's instructions.

There was a skinny guy who looked about twelve, but I knew from Sunday he was seventeen and a Life Scout whose name was Ed Mitchell. He was doing pretty well but I couldn't resist reaching out and closing my hand around the middle of his paddle. "Here, see, if you keep your right arm perfectly straight and keep it like that when you come down for your stroke into the water it'll slip in like a knife and without any splash . . . pull down, keep it straight . . . there. Perfect."

"Thanks," he said, not at all pissed off at receiving instruction from a Star Scout younger than himself. "That was helpful."

I'd hoped to spend some time in the tower talking with Bart, but when I turned that way, he was gone and Bill Platte, the third member of the waterfront crew, officially called the "Director" (who wasn't a lifeguard either), occupied Bart's spot and was checking out things he was responsible for: the canoes, paddles, paddleboards, boats, oars, life jackets, and other stuff that they kept careful track of.

I got back to the tent around four, just as the guys were coming in from hiking, all sweaty and either weary or faking it—except for Curly, who seemed more animated than when he'd left on the hike.

Andy was likewise full of high spirits: "We did it, Larry," Andy said, eyes gleaming. "Wore me out, but it was the first time a hike was ever fun." Poteet had already left for his tent, but Curly came up to me and punched me in the shoulder. "Hey!"

"Hey yourself," I said, and punched him back lightly, about as hard as he'd punched me. Then somehow we were grappling with our arms, each trying to get the other in a hold. And somehow as we stood there struggling with each other it became serious, and we edged a bit away from our tent into a little bare place in front of it where we'd have some room to maneuver.

We circle now, arms reaching out, legs dancing as we seek an opening, then we come together, heads forced into the notch of each other's neck and shoulder—never has Curly seemed so tall—and our arms vie for solid purchase—when suddenly Curly shoots his legs back, and with a long arm reaches way back and grabs the back of my left leg just above the knee—and pulls up on it—

We dance around, he more balanced than me, and—

—he drops to his knees, jerking me toward and then over his humped back, dumping me on my mass . . . he stands, winded but triumphant.

I get creakily up, spitting out a few pine needles, my ears burning—and somewhere a red wire is switched on in my head—

He comes at me fast, whirls just before contact so his back slams hard into my chest—then facing the direction I am, he swings an arm around, wedging it between my left arm and shoulder and uses his superior leverage to send me sprawling to the dirt once again . . .

—this time I am a bit more pissed and we come again into another clinch, grappling and probing for the other's weak spot: since I'm stronger I'm able to clamp fingers of both my hands around his upper arms where they join his shoulder and squeeze, deep, hard, feeling my thumbs going deep into his biceps just below his armpits. . . . Curly's so startled that before he can make another move I'm able to loop my right foot around and kick his left out from under him, and he goes down, me riding him all the way, and when he hits the ground he gives a loud *oof*!

I shove myself off, quickly stand, dance around him a little, ready to go as soon as he regains his footing.

But Curly rolls slowly over on his back, then sits up as if it takes all his strength. His face is white and he's gasping, but he puts out a hand to me and I take it and pull him upright, where he towers over me, shuddering and getting his wind back . . . there are pine needles and fragments of dead leaf in his hair, which is standing up wirily all around his head.

"Wow, hey, you're pretty good, Curly," I say. "Where'd'ya pick up all those nifty moves? You gotta teach me some of that stuff . . ."

His breathing's getting better. "Switzerland," he says.

That evening after dinner most of us stayed in the Lodge for a presentation on knot-tying—everyone knew Perky had a special affection for knots—and I was one of the few watching carefully when Ed Gentry appeared before us, just himself, no diagrams or slide show of different knots, just a Kroger shopping bag filled with a bunch of lengths of clothesline, say two and a half feet per piece, which he distributed. He kept one for himself. His only other prop was a round chunk of firewood, probably for use with knots like half-hitches and sheet bends. I happened to be interested in knots. Gentry was a small man in his forties, wiry and tanned.

Perky sat at a table to our rear, no doubt keeping an eye on our responses.

The others seemed bored, but I liked it as Gentry went through the best-known knots, demonstrating each twice in slow motion, then a third in normal time, demonstrating overhand knots, a draw-loop, Ashley's stopper knot, and then he came suddenly to my favorite, the bowline. "Even though it may not be the strongest loop knot nor is it terrifically secure if you're using stiff or slippery rope," Gentry said, "it's been rightly called 'the king of knots,' and it can be used in a host of applications—and of course can be especially important in enterprises like mountain climbing and sailing." He lifted his head and looked directly into my eyes: "Fellas, if your rope's sound and your execution's proper, a good knot'll never let you down as certain other things are bound to do . . ."

I'd made my own bowline, pronounced "bo-linn," right along with him. I tested it now, and no matter how hard I pulled I couldn't make the loop slip. I was pretty good at knots myself, seemed to sense in them something, some purpose or other, that went beyond what knots were supposed to be for.

Ed Gentry's demonstration only took about twenty minutes and when he finished, he had a little surprise for us: "Well, fellows, it's getting close to nine and my bedtime. And I know you always sing a song together before parting, but tonight I'd like to introduce a man who, as you already know, has an extremely fine baritone, Camp Director L. Perkins Gibb, who'll sing a Stephen Foster favorite to conclude things. "Lovell," he said, "come up and take the stage."

Those of us who had been at Camp G previously were dumbstruck, then did a series of Lucille-Ball-Desi-Arnaz gawking double takes for each other: Scouts had long wondered what the L stood for. (Loren? Lesley? Leroy?)

Perky ambled to the front of the room, lanky and well-coordinated, grinning, not at all flustered at what we figured was a slip by

Gentry. "Well, there you have it, gentlemen, now you know. And no, Ed didn't slip up; I just thought it was time to get the damned name out in the open and end a lot of needless and idle speculation. And now, gentlemen, if you'll permit me, I shall sing for the supper I've eaten with you earlier."

He stood and began to sing, making absolutely no motion, his arms still at his sides, his palms turned slightly outward:

"Gone are the days
When my heart was
Young and gay"

His voice was deep and startling, liquid, more bass than baritone, and suddenly I could see that ancient black man sitting on a boulder, looking up at the moon, white-haired and rheumatic, maybe the last of his line, looking up at the gleaming moon through an old apple tree's appallingly twisted black limbs, ready at least to die:

"I'm coming, I'm coming,
For my head is bending low
I hear those gentle voices
Calling Old Black Joe . . ."

The last words seemed to hang in the air after Perky'd ceased singing, and for long seconds nobody moved or said anything. Then the dozen or so of us clapped raggedly.

Curly and I lay on our cots in our sleeping bags in the dark. It must have been around ten. We'd been over in Poteet and Andy's tent for a while. Everybody seemed tired and on the verge of nodding off and the talk had been mostly of the hiking, and how Nick was a hard taskmaster—"a real bastard," I was surprised to hear Andy call him. Maybe he'd picked it up from Poteet.

"My dad'll maybe be coming for Waterfront Night," Curly said.

"Really? What's your father do?"

"He's what you call an efficiency expert. He goes all around Europe to these different firms, these companies, and he makes a study, and then he tells them what they need to do to be more efficient . . . takes a special kind of person. So what's the story on your father?"

"He died in the war."

"Wow. Man, I'm really sorry to hear that—you mean Korea?" I was surprised: he really *did* look like he was sorry—sorry and concerned that my dad had been killed nine years ago, the first sign I'd seen that he could care about someone or something other than himself.

"Nah—World War Two."

"Wow. Well, shit, Larry, that's a hell of a tough break . . ." His pupils looked bottomless with concern.

"Yeah." I couldn't think of a damn thing to say.

Maybe I should have told him how I sometimes got out photos of my dad, Delbert Carstairs, and sat with them on my lap, gazing for long minutes: I particularly liked one from the '20s showing him in tennis togs, grinning in the sun, his racket resting jauntily over his shoulder like a rifle. And the somber photo of him in his army uniform, staring stonily into the camera.

"Larry, what do you think of me—really?"

"Uh, well, um, how do you mean?"

"You know, like what kind of a person do I *seem* to you? A good one? A bad one? A nice guy? A creep? A prick? Am I basically okay, do you think? Or fucked-up in some way maybe you can see but I can't? Like maybe because I'm an only child like you and I don't always feel too much for other people nor understand how they feel? Hah! You know, they think I'm fourteen but actually I'm going on seventeen."

"Well . . . gosh, I don't know, Curly, it's hard to say, but . . . but, yeah, you *seem* like a real good guy—the kinda guy you can probably, you know, get to trust, and count on in a pinch. 'Course all's I know's your surface . . . takes a long time to get to know any guy real well . . . I got a coupla friends at home named Miller and Doc, oh, and Alex, that I've known all my life and I don't know if I really know them all that well . . . sometimes I think I do, sometimes

I don't . . ." As my voice trailed off, I could feel myself blush. "Say, did you really mean it that you picked up those wrestling tricks in Switzerland? Were you serious?"

"Oh, yes." He looked annoyed at my change of subject.

"Well, it's nifty—you're really good."

"Well, maybe I could be but for one thing. No, two things."

"Like what?"

"Inclination and stamina. As you could probably already perceive."

"Yeah? Really?"

"Yeah, really—it's mainly on account of I got something called Marfan's syndrome."

He might as well have said hoovus-goovus.

"Yeah?"

"Yeah—y'know what that is?"

"No."

"Something they think Lincoln—you know, ole Honest Abe—had. Ya got long limbs, long fingers, sometimes you're double-jointed, like I happen to be . . . and you're likely not gonna make it much past forty, that is if you're that lucky . . . so if I seem kinda different to you, Larry, it's not so much 'cause'a my screwy upbringing—my dad's always had mistresses since he got divorced when I was five—but 'cause I may not gonna be around all that much longer . . . also I got an aortic aneurysm . . ."

Time to change the subject again: "Well . . . so except for alla that, how'd you like Switzerland? How come you went to school there? D'jou speak Swiss?"

He laughed, and it was a good sound, genuine and hearty: "Christ's teeth, Larry, you're my kinda guy, you don't get all sentimental about stuff, you want to know, understand, how things are . . . you're all right!" And he laughed delightedly.

"I am?"

"Damn straight! And yes, I speak French, sort of, and just a little Swiss-German, enough to get by, and a little Spanish . . ."

I waited for him to answer about Switzerland, but he acted as if he already had.

Then he said, "Y'know, Larry, knowing you're gonna be doing well to reach thirty-five or forty gives ya a different outlook than you'd otherwise have . . ."

"Yeah?"

"Yeah."

"Like how?"

"Well, you read any of the nineteenth-century Russians?"

"Me? Naw—like who?"

"How's about Chekhov. Tolstoy. Dostoevsky. Turgenev."

"No." I'd only heard of Tolstoy.

"Well, this guy in Dostoevsky's *The Brothers K*, Ee-vonn, concludes that if there's no God, then all's permissible—you know, anything goes . . . or not goes, who cares, steal something or kill somebody, it doesn't matter 'cause everything means about the same, there is no moral order, y'see—hey, the ultimate laissez faire, huh? Well, Larry, I sure as hell don't believe there's a God nor anything else in particular in charge of the stupid universe, so I don't really follow any whatcha'd call rules and laws especially, Larry, except to do and say whatever works to get by. But I practically always take the easiest way . . . unless there's something I *really* want. But there's something to be said for choosing the path of least resistance, you know . . . kinda Dowism-like?"

He'd lost me. "So what do you really want, most of all?"

"Oh," he said vaguely, "lotsa things, I guess . . . then maybe then again, not so much. Lemme tell you, I don't need money, or any kinds of *things*, maybe that's 'cause in my position I can pretty much get 'em just by asking . . . guess what I most want is a one really true friend, somebody I can completely trust, you know, someone who doesn't try to queer you when you drop the soap in the shower—someone I can tell the things about me nobody else knows and he can do the same deal with me. So then it'd be kinda the two of us sort of taking up arms against the universe, at least in some minor way, not that anything really means anything . . . y'know?"

"Hmmm. You talkin' male or female?"

"Oh, Christ, *male*—I don't think there's a female alive can be really *trusted* . . . even if you happen to love 'em—I think almost all women are naturally queer anyhow . . ."

"You think Andy might be such a guy?"

Curly's laugh was harsh and explosive in the near-dark: "Christ's teeth, Larry! You must be kidding. He's a babe in the woods. Possibly a fruit. Naw, I was thinking of someone like you, Larry: you maybe don't know all that much yet but you're awful good raw material, and of course you're an only child like me . . . y'know, Larry, there's a story of Chekhov's I like a lot called 'Misery'—see, there's this hackie in nineteenth-century Russia whose son has just died, and now he has to take these drunken swine around in his carriage: they cheat and abuse him, but even so he keeps trying to tell them about his son. It's pitiful. The drunkards couldn't care less, Larry! Well, hell, finally, the hackie comes back to the livery, tired and broke, and there's nobody there he can express his grief to either . . . so finally, at long last, he gets up off his pallet and goes out in the dark to the stable where his little mare is. He's made no money so it's hay instead of oats for her tonight. Anyway, like I say, he goes to the stable and feeds the little mare some hay, feeling her warm breath on his hands. And the last sentence is, 'Iona is carried away and tells her all about it.'"

His voice was very low and sad, and I'd bet his eyes were glistening.

I made a vow to read the story sometime.

Four

O n Tuesday morning a little before nine I was up in Bart's tower, keeping an eye on things. He'd take over at nine on the dot, but he liked to get in a little fly-tying first thing in the morning: "Seems to clear my head a little, y'know?" He was extremely good at performing delicate tasks with his fingers.

Several Swimmers were at the moment bobbing amid floats on the lines defining their space.

But even back in the guardshack Bart always positioned himself so he could peer out a window every minute or so and check on things. It was always dim in the guardshack, and when you entered after being in the sun you could hardly see; it was low-ceilinged and one whole wall was covered with oars, paddles, life jackets, buoys, and ropes, all suspended from wooden pegs.

And here came Andy, shuffling up in his yellow trunks with orange seahorses, a towel over his shoulder, stepping gingerly as he came upon a patch of gravel before the walkway down to the waterfront.

"Hiya, Andy!" I called down to him, and his upturned face broke into a huge smile and his eyes lit up—I was always cheered when someone seemed happy to see me, and I smiled back. The sun caught his burr head so that it glowed.

"Hiya, Larry—hey, you think they might let me do a retest this morning? To see if I can maybe move up to Intermediate?"

"Yeah, sure, I bet they will—be right there, I'll go hunt up Bart."

I left my towel, Sea & Ski and *Scout Field Book* on the plank seat I used—when Bart was there, he sat on a folding metal auditorium chair catty-corner from my plank (and always on a cushion: "Confucius say, 'He who has piles has plenty,' Larry . . ."), his 7x35 binoculars hanging just above his head from a nail in one of the uprights that supported the roof—and swiftly skinned down the tower, swinging showily around an upright at the bottom.

"Aw, hey, you don't have to go to any trouble, Larry, I can go find him . . . or just wait for him here . . ."

"Hey, us guys from Ermine Falls gotta stick together—stay there, I'll be right back . . ."

I waited a few seconds in the guardshack until objects began to appear like shapes on photo paper in a developing bath.

Bart was seated at a table heaped with piles of Camp G brochures—he'd cleared himself a little space for his fly-tying equipment and he was moodily tinkering with his automatic H-R fly rod reel, turning the crosshatched cylinder clockwise to wind the mechanism, then pushing on the little finger lever and watching the spool spin. It made a spooky whir in the gloom.

"Hey, Bart, you got time to give my pal Andy from home a quick swim test to see if he can move up a notch?"

"Buddy, a pal of yours is a pal of mine."

It was a nice day and Bart was pleasant to Andy, who unfortunately failed the test, though I could see he'd improved a lot since the first one: he didn't splash so much, didn't gasp as much, and his movements weren't as jerky as before, but I'd doubted from the outset he'd be up to Bart's standards.

Bart took him aside, and I was able to hear: "Hey, Andy, buddy, a little better, but 'fraid you're just gonna have to linger as a Beginner just a little longer there, pard, but you're not that far off, you're coming along—so whyn'tcha work a little with Larry, and we'll give it another shot tomorrow morning, whaddaya say?"

I take Andy aside, and we go over to the western shoreline where I shake the sand off the square of paint-stained canvas I've brought along that we use for dry demonstrations.

I get down on the canvas, lie on my right side: "Okay, Andy, let's have a go at the sidestroke—see, you gotta coordinate your movements sorta like this, ya bring your left leg up for a stroke-kick, and as you do, you reach up like this with your right arm, like you're picking cherries, then you bring it down like this, meantime you're bringing your left hand up, making a little circle with it around your cherry-picking hand . . . like this . . . your right arm shoots out again at the same time you're kicking your left leg out and drawing the right up under you . . . here, you try it dry now, lemme see how it looks, then we'll go try it in the water."

Sun catches the lake's surface so beams shoot into your eyes when you hold your head a certain way: when they do, it takes a while for the dark sun spots to fade.

Andy lowers himself onto the canvas, now stained with my sweat: "I don't know why, but I guess water just scares me for some reason, Larry," Andy says, more to himself than to me, looking off across the lake. "It just makes me feel kinda . . . uh, you know, jelly-belly-like, sort of . . ." He seems to be looking at the far shore where the foliage, shaded from the sun, is so dark it's almost black.

When we finished, it was close to lunchtime so I decided to walk back to the pod with Andy.

"Hey, pal," I said, "you did a whole lot better in the water after a few dry runs—I think you're ready. Come back tomorrow morning and take another crack at it with Bart . . ."

"You really think I can make it?" Andy looked doubtful, was chewing his lower lip and starting to trudge rather than walk.

"Absolutely. Maybe Bart'll even bump you up to Swimmer, who knows?" I slowed my steps to match his.

"God, that'd be great. Say, uh, Larry . . . can I ask ya something . . . whaddaya think of Curly?"

I'd have been evasive if he hadn't looked so earnest: "I . . . well, I dunno . . . y'know, he seems like a nifty guy, y'know, and he's really bright and's been around, but can't say's I really know him all that well . . . he's gone to school in Switzerland, seems to know all kindsa things, speaks French, reads a lot, stuff like that . . . be interesting to see what his parents are like, if they come tomorrow to Waterfront Night, that is . . ."

"Oh," Andy said quickly, "Curly just has his father: he told me his mother died two years ago—she had a congenital heart condition, he said."

"You don't say. Well, anyhow, so whadda *you* think of him?" I wondered which version was true: his parents divorced when Curly was five, or his mother died recently. Maybe neither was.

Andy blushed: "Well, he's just about the neatest guy I ever knew, Larry . . . he just stands there in the sun and it glints off the hair on his arms and hands and legs . . . he looks like he belongs in a movie, like he'd be really good in something like *Kidnapped* or *Swiss Family Robinson* or something like that . . ." Andy's look was faraway, and he restlessly slapped his hand against a pine tree as we walked on.

I was waiting for him to say more but he didn't.

Then he realized I expected something from him: "Curly offered to teach me to swim better too, Larry, he's so good I don't know why I didn't take him up on it . . ." He blushed again, deep and red. "I didn't mean that you aren't real good at this yourself, of course . . ."

"Yeah, Curly seems pretty good at whatever he does—you can probably learn a lot about swimming from him too . . . probably lots of other stuff too."

"Do you trust him?"

I was struck; actually, now that Andy's mentioned it, I did sort of trust Curly, even though he'd clearly lied about the deal with his mother to one of us. Or, it occurred to me again, maybe he'd lied to both of us. "I dunno . . . kinda, I guess . . ."

"That's what I think too. There's not many guys you trust right from the start . . ."

I glanced at the sun. "Hey, getting close to noon, guess they'll play on Soupie-Soupie-Soupie in a minute or two, huh? I better get back to the pod and get dressed for lunch."

"Yeah, me too. This wet suit itches."

I found myself disappointing Curly again when he and Poteet got back from hiking in midafternoon (they'd only done five miles): "Shit," he said, "goddamnit, Larry, I was really counting on you, the fucking irony was so delicious—I mean, a real Curly and a real Larry, each playing a fake Larry and a fake Curly and then Andy doing Moe . . ."

"Yeah, I was looking forward to it myself . . . I like acting, I've acted in all our school plays . . . but, see, Bart's got this safety thing—he wants me to demonstrate the new way they do artificial respiration now . . . thinks it could save lives . . ."

"Well, shit."

"Hey, ask Poteet—have him be Curly, and Andy can be Moe and you can be Larry . . ."

"Yeah, but I wanted the *real* names to correspond, ya know? It's the *irony* of the thing, you see, the essential irony."

"Yeah, but that'd likely do the trick—I mean, I'd really like to do it myself but I promised Bart . . ."

"Yeah yeah yeah," Curly said, but I could see him already imagining and adjusting to my suggestion. "So what's with this new artificial respiration deal?"

"Well, basically, steada straddling the drowned guy's back with your knees and pushing down on his lower back just below his rib cage, ya kneel down in front of him, lean forward, press down hard but slow where ya would the other way, but then you lean back and as ya do, you slide your hands up along the guy's or girl's upper arms from armpit to elbow, lifting 'em up sorta like wings . . . helps force any water out and stimulate breathing at the same time . . ."

"Show me."

"Okay. I can use another practice run."

He put a blanket on the bald ground not far from our tent's entrance and I got down on my knees, facing Curly, prone before me.

His taut back muscles quivered at my touch and when I pressed harder down low on his upper back, Curly groaned. I pressed harder; his skin was smooth and the long muscles under it almost rigid. I pulled up on his long sinewy upper arms, lifting as much as I could before discomfort made him flinch.

I was counting one-thousand-one, one-thousand-two as I pushed and lifted, shooting for about twenty movements a minute. After a time, Curly seemed almost asleep under my hands, so I stopped. "Thanks," I said, "think I got the timing just about right."

Curly got up, taking deep breaths. "Well, I b'lieve you cleaned out my lungs, Larry, hell, maybe my liver too, who knows . . ." He was grinning, looked happy. "You give a great massage, Larry. I feel like a new woman already."

Later that afternoon, while the others were practicing their Three Stooges routine, I got up and wandered along the North Trail until I came to the deserted archery range.

I sat on a bale of hay and looked at the huge round target next to me, now peppered with holes, very few of which were near the black center ring. There seemed absolutely no one in the vicinity at the moment. Nearby, squirrels gibbered and an angry blue jay's cries pierced the air from time to time.

A chipmunk came around from behind a hemlock, saw me, stopped dead, eyes bright, tail twitching, then disappeared.

Now I was wishing I hadn't got hooked into the goddamn artificial respiration thing—it would've been a hell of a lot more fun to play a Stooge, out bumbling around, slapping and getting slapped, and best of all letting loose with the *Ny-yuck-ny-yuck-ny-yuck*s I wanted.

That evening at the amphitheater, the three came bumbling out looking pretty good, each wearing a white busboy's jacket borrowed from the kitchen intended to let you know they were doctors, and they were doing a pretty good job of bumping into each other, delivering many nose pinches, elbow digs, and cuffs to the backs of heads. "*Ny-yuck! Ny-yuck, ny-yuck!*" they went and I envied them.

I was surprised how well they filled the Stooge roles: Curly was Larry, which sort of fit because his spiraling curls had something of the aspect of Larry's corkscrew clown curls; as Moe, Andy's overgrown crewcut had something of the mushroom shape of Moe's crown of black hair; and Poteet fit Curly pretty well—he'd really gotten into the role, even making his muscular body a bit pear-shaped to complete the illusion by stuffing a pillow under his jacket, and his almost-to-the-skin crewcut gave him a certain resemblance to the original. And he had a pretty lusty *Nyuck! Nyuck! Nyuck!*

Along with their Stooge-like bumbling they had been carrying about and abusing a life-size dummy they'd apparently cobbled together from sweat clothes stuffed with hay—probably stolen from the archery range—so it looked more scarecrow than dying patient.

Now with great ceremony, they laid their patient-dummy on his back, elbowing each other in the guts and smacking foreheads, all the while keeping up with a steady stream of *Ny-yuck! Ny-yuck! Ny-yuck!*

It was a little hard to get it, but I finally understood the doctors were arguing about whether the patient had a tumor or cancer.

"*Cancer!*" cries Larry (Curly).

Smack! A cuff to Curly's head.

"*Tumor!*" cries Moe (Andy).

Whap! An elbow in the guts from Larry.

Whack! Cuff! Elbow! goes Curly (Poteet), unable to suppress a huge grin as he pokes the other two mercilessly.

And of course: *Nyuck-nyuck-nyuck!*

After the clowning, Larry and Moe get down on their knees and as Curly looks on they appear to be groping around in the dummy's abdominal cavity. Suddenly Larry stands, holding aloft a number ten can of pork and beans, turning the can so all may see the label, and he shrieks out: "*Can*-sir!"

Moe then reaches deeper into the body and pulls out two smaller cans of pork and beans and, standing, shrills: "*Two-mer!*"

The audience is silent for a couple seconds as the joke sinks in, then uneven applause and even a few hisses.

Then it was my turn on stage. Steve Crawley had agreed to play the drowned victim. He was turning out to be a lot friendlier than the pasty Ned Fangbone, who always looked sour and resentful whenever Steve was in conversation with anyone other than himself. So I'd been pleased yesterday when Andy and Poteet were talking in front of Steve and Ned's tent and Ned had come up and pushed Andy out of the way of the tent's entrance. Poteet had swiftly pivoted and clamped one hand around Ned's fleshy left upper arm. He squeezed until Ned went "*Wah!*", a child's cry of pain and surprise. "Excuse me, asswipe," Poteet said calmly, "I believe you owe my friend Andy an apology." Andy's face turned white at the small violence.

"I'm sorry," Ned said through gritted teeth.

"Sure thing," Andy said, face finally turning red.

Jim released Ned and turned back to Andy: "Let's see, what were we saying before the interruption?"

Steve and I took over the center of the amphitheater where our pod-mates had just done their slapstick.

Steve lay prone, stretching his arms out in front of him, and I knelt in the dirt before him, shifting a bit because bits of gravel were pressing into my knees. I looked up at the audience gathered together in a clump on bleachers in the northwest corner. There were only about a dozen Scouts left now, and they were dwarfed by this amphitheater meant to accommodate an audience of a couple hundred. But I knew that Fangbone was probably haunting some obscure corner just out of sight—he got surly and watchful whenever Steve's attention was engaged by anyone other than himself.

Just as I had done earlier in the day with Curly, I bent over Steve pressing down, counting one-thousand-one, one-thousand-two, pulling Steve's arms up and spreading them to force water from his lungs.

When I finished, we both stood and I called out, "Exactly twenty compressions in one minute!" There was a second or two of restless applause, then a high tinny voice screamed "*Yo!*" And Skit Night was concluded.

Back at the pod, Curly and I lay on our cots, he inside his light-weight sleeping bag, me lying on top of my bag (rated for 32 de-grees). Its puffy nylon felt slippery as wet satin on my back.

"Hey, Larry, how's about a beer?"

"Why, sure thing, Curly—we can just hitchhike into Traverse'n go down to Little Bohemia on East Front and get plastered . . .'

"Very funny. However, Sport, I gotta coupla cans stashed by the archery range. Whaddya say?"

"You do?"

"Yeah. Whaddya say?"

"Ny-yuck, ny-yuck!"

"Let's go, ole pard."

"Yippee-eye-eh-oh-ki-yay!" And we slouched off into the night, almost giggling.

Behind a large oak in the woods about ten feet from the trail, Curly removes a twig sticking straight up from the ground and begins to dig with his hands, the loose earth and its covering of leaves coming away easily.

"Voilà!" And sure enough he comes up with two earth-covered cans of Budweiser: "The King of Beers, Larry. I got the other four cans buried around here. Dirt keeps'em cool and outta sight." He takes a bandana from the pocket of his shorts and wipes them off, then uses it to clean dirt from his hands. He takes a church key from a pocket and sings, "Be prepared, that's the Boy Scouts march-ing song . . ."

"Yeah, I see you're prepared all right."

"D'jou know Nick and Irwin are queer?"

"Aw, c'mon . . .'

"No shit, I'm serious . . ."

"Yeah? Well, how d'ya know?"

"It was yesterday when we hiked—it was just a little look at first, Irwin'd look over at Nick and he wiggled his ass so delicate-like it'd've been easy to miss and later on I saw Nick give Irwin a little pat on the ass . . ."

"Yeah, so what, athletes do that all the time . . ."

"I can tell, I tellya—I got a kind of sixth sense with stuff like this." *Phht*: the church key pierces the first can. Curly makes a small hole, then a bigger one on the opposite side. He does the same to the other can, hands it to me.

He hoists his can aloft. "Well, Larry, here's to—"

He stops, lowers his arm. We can hear someone coming along the trail. Curly puts a finger to his lips and we both slide around the tree until we're on the side away from the trail and our backs are pressed against the rough bark of the oak's bole.

I clutch my full can carefully, fearfully.

"*Shit!*" someone cries, not far from the tree.

"Well, watch where you're going, dumbass."

The first speaker was Irwin, the second Nick.

"Aw, fuck you. Your ass sucks buttermilk."

"You oughta know."

They can't be more than six feet away.

"How about a little goose?" Nick asks, and Irwin gives a kind of squawk. "Like that? Now how'd ya like a little gander?"

"Yeah . . . here?"

"Well, lemme tellya, this ain't the place. And back in the woods here there's fuckin' poison ivy all over—don't want no fungus on my sweet young bungus . . ."

"Well, then, where?"

"I dunno, but this ain't it, let's think on it on the way back . . ."

When we're sure they're gone, Curly and I let out our breath at the same time and laugh nervously because we did.

I wonder if there really is poison ivy here. But there just seems to be leaves covering bare ground beneath the great oak.

"Howya like them apples?" Curly asks. "See, I toldya so."

"Okay, so you win, you're a genius."

"Damn straight I am. Let's see, where was I? Oh, yeah . . ." He hoists his can of beer: "Here's to ya, Larry . . . no, here's to the both of us, expert queer spotters that we are." We bring cans to mouth, drink.

Five minutes later we've both finished our beers. I'd had sips before but never a whole can. "Ah," Curly said, "that's a little bit better, eh?"

I laughed for no reason. I felt lightheaded and loose and like I could swim forever if I were out on Lake G right now. "Right!" I said.

"Well, this shit's for the birds, fuck ole Mother Nature, let's cut out of here . . . ya know, there're any number of ways I could screw those two fruits up from here to Sunday if I wanted to . . ."

"Yeah? Like how?"

"Well, f'rinstance I could send Perky an anonymous note. Or I could put a note on the waterfront bulletin board. Nah, that'd be too easy. First, just for fun, I might sneak into their tent and put a jar of Vaseline with broken light bulb glass in it on each of their pillows, just to give'em a little thrill and let'em know somebody's onto 'em . . . oh, I could dream up an infinite number of ways if I really wanted to nail them, Larry . . ."

"Are you going to?"

"Nah, not right now anyhow. I mean, why bother? What'd it get me? What'd be the point: How'd it make *my* lot better? What'd be *my* payoff?"

"You got a point there," I said.

"Sometimes it pays to be practical," Curly said. "Like, you know, pragmatic, à la old William James."

I was just about to coast into sleep that night when Curly started up again . . . I was a little groggy and seemed to have missed the set-up: ". . . and so then these three guys go down to the local whorehouse, where they start checking out the quiff and this little sawed-off one goes up to this big boogie whore with huge thighs and gigantic tits, and he says, 'I'll take *you,* there, Sally-Lou . . .' 'Oh yeah,' says she, 'well, let's have us a little short-arm inspection first, there, Slick, so haul'er out!' He does, and he's got this tiny little needledick, y'see. The whore looks at it and busts out laughing: 'Why you little dip-shit, who do you think you're gonna satisfy with *that* little dingus?' By now the little guy's just jumping up and down he's so horny: '*Me!*' he hollers, '*Me! Me! Me!*' "

And just as on Sunday night, I dissolved into laughter, but this time it was so shudderingly wild I couldn't be sure I wasn't also weeping.

Earlier in the day, I'd been in our tent changing from my trunks into shorts and had happened to see a flash of movement over by Andy and Poteet's tent. Andy and Curly both wore trunks, and apparently Curly had been instructing Andy in getting his move-ments right in the sidestroke, but now they were still and one of Curly's long-fingered golden hands rested on Andy's pale arm. He briefly stroked Andy's bicep, murmuring something Andy found comforting, for his pleasant round face went smooth with pleasure.

Five

Wednesday morning a little before nine I was back up in Bart's tower, checking on the requirements in my *Scout Handbook* for the hiking merit badge when I was startled to see Curly and Andy headed my way, both in trunks, both with towels identically tossed over their shoulders. They were in high spirits, walking so close their bare arms occasionally brushed, and Curly looped his left arm around Andy's shoulders and gave him an encouraging squeeze: "You can do it, kiddo, I got faith in you."

"Okay, then," Andy said, looking up gratefully at Curly, "I'll give it all I got."

"Sure you will. Hiya, Larry . . ."

"Hey . . . guys . . ."

"Hi, Larry."

"Say, is one of the lifeguards around, Larry? Andy oughta clear Swimmer this time, don'tcha think, between the two of us working him over, he's primed and ready . . . locked and loaded, aren'tcha, Andy?"

"You bet!" Andy's eagerness and new confidence looked genuine. He almost glowed.

"Lemme go ask Bart, he's in the guardshack. He'll probably do it." I nipped down the ladder.

Bart was seated at his worktable working on a fly with bits of bright yellow threaded through gray stuff held in his tiny vise.

"Hey, Bart . . . thinkya could maybe check out this guy from my hometown troop one more time? Andy? The Beginner you tested again yesterday and he didn't make Intermediate? But I think me'n Curly's got him up to where he might make it this time around . . ."

Bart yawned, wound some thread loosely around the dainty fly in his vise, put down a hemostat he was using, leaving the ends dangling. "Sure thing."

He got up, scratching his brown corrugated stomach, tiger-striped from the sun, yawning. "Okay, Doctor, where's the patient?"

Curly stood by Bart like an encouraging parent as Andy prepared to enter the water. I went down to my usual spot by the dock's dogleg, though not for any real reason other than to observe since Bart had the clipboard.

This time Andy didn't jump in feet first, but dove in; there was a resounding slap when his belly hit the water, but all in all it wasn't bad.

"You can do it, Andy!" Curly called as Andy surfaced—and Andy did do pretty well this time, sidestroking down to the dogleg, turning fairly smoothly and heading back, sidestroking on his other side, and when he knew he was getting better he began digging his hands a little deeper into the water and putting a little more snap into his scissor kick.

Andy was grinning broadly when he climbed the ladder. One way or another, Curly'd helped Andy find some self-confidence.

Bart put an arm around Andy's shoulders and gave him a squeeze: "Way to go, there, Ace, not so hot on the way down but *very* strong coming back—congrats, I declare that henceforth you're a Swimmer. I'll have Larry make the change on your disk on the board."

"Thanks." Andy's eyes widened and he smiled broadly with relief and pleasure; Curly gave him a cuff on the back of his head. "Good show, kid, good show!"

Curly turned to Bart, using his friendliest manner: "Say, do you suppose Andy and I could maybe take a quick swim in the Swimmer area just to kind of celebrate? A victory lap or two?"

Andy's ears twitched at the word "celebrate," and he kept smiling.

I was amazed all over again about how easily Curly could get his way with people without ever having to really work at it, and how just about everybody, myself included, seemed to instantly like and respond to him.

"Yeah, sure thing, go do about ten, fifteen minutes. Hey, after all, with Larry in the tower, what could go wrong, huh?" Bart winked at me. "You *are* gonna watch over'em, right, Larry?"

"Sure thing."

They entered the water tentatively from the shore, stepping carefully over the rocky bottom, then swimming in lazy breaststrokes out to where buoys on a rope divided the Intermediate from the Swimmer area. The formerly clumsy Andy now looked almost seal-like as he stroked along, Curly swimming alongside, duplicating his strokes . . . for some reason I thought of *The Creature from the Black Lagoon*: the girl lazily swimming on the surface, while just below her, almost touching her at times and mimicking her movements, swam Gill Man, goggling at her flashing white legs.

Earlier I'd promised Curly I'd do the hike with the rest of the pod today. We'd leave around eleven, all of us getting bagged lunches from the kitchen—it was going to be a short one, five or six miles. But now I regretted it, hated to exchange soothing water for sweaty mucking around in the woods.

I climbed up onto the tower and sat on the bench catty-cornered from Bart, who was gingerly adjusting his bottom to his cushion. This was pretty much what I'd done last year, avoiding crafts and archery and that kind of stuff and trying not to draw attention to myself as I hung around the waterfront. Soon I'd been spending well over half the day hanging out in the guard tower or guardshack.

Just after I'd inked in black and red half-moons on Andy's disk, certifying him a Swimmer, Bud came out of the guardshack and went scrambling up the tower rungs like a monkey, looking jubilant: "My baby's coming! Just got the call at the camp office in the Lodge. She oughta be turning up any minute!" he exclaimed to Bart. Bart grinned and gave him a thumbs-up.

The hike was on one of the several trails leading through the wooded countryside, going up a grade for a while, then descending, and it felt good to move along at a good-enough clip to bring out a light sweat. I sort of wished I had hiking boots, but my tennis shoes were doing okay.

We could hear the faint *snap . . . snap . . . snap* from the rifle range, where Sergeant Exley would be instructing in the use of single-shot bolt-action .22s and Scouts would be firing shorts from eleven until noon. As far as I could tell, nobody had much interest in the archery range—the same targets were on the hay bales with no new holes in them.

Curly started to sing,

"Oh, I walked down Canal Street
I knocked at every door,
But I'll be goddamned, sir,
If I could find a whore . . ."

But no one else knew it or seemed to much appreciate it so he knocked it off.

A glowering Nick led the way; he'd cut a small maple sapling with his Scout knife, and now used it to aimlessly whack foliage on either side of the trail as we passed by.

Irwin sulkily trudged at the rear—clearly something was amiss between them. I could almost hear Curly's voice in my ear: *Christ, Larry whatcha think queers do anyhow—y'know there's only so many things ya* can *do: ya can stick your dick in somebody's mouth or asshole or vice versa* . . . thinking about it made me queasy.

I thought of Bud crying out that his baby was coming, and how, a few minutes later, the guys all gawked when a young woman had driven up in a new bright red Chevy convertible, top down, and parked close to the guardshack. She was plump and blond, wore a summery aquamarine dress that glistened like oil, bright red lipstick, a beautiful tan, several gold bracelets; a wide purple band across her forehead kept her long shining hair out of her face. I'd gawked like all the rest. "Wow!" someone'd muttered behind me. And Bud came out of the guardshack glowing, freshly showered and dressed in chinos and tennis shirt. He got into the car's passenger side, and they pulled away, leaving our imaginations to endlessly spin their wheels.

Sun through foliage fell blotchily on me, Curly, Andy, and Poteet as we passed glumly beneath stands of canopying maples. After a mile on our northerly route, maples diminished and oak, hemlock, birch, and pine became more abundant. There were plenty of squirrels and birds, chiefly raucous blue jays, but nothing else interesting in the way of wildlife. A northwest breeze blew across the trail, cooling and soothing and carrying a hint of Lake Greavey as we marched glumly on. I'd thought Steve Crawley and Ned Fangbone were coming, but they didn't show.

Whatever was going on between Nick and Irwin seemed to have spread sourness among the rest of us and we didn't sing, chatter, or horse around much.

Nick, supposedly a naturalist, found only one thing to stop for and explain, a clutch of wizened morels left from spring. "Here you go, guys, morel mushrooms, see, easily recognizable and safe to eat . . . don't eat any other kinda mushrooms 'less you know exactly what they are and that they're edible . . . you can get something a lot worse than the drizzlin' shits if you bite into the wrong kind, lemme tell ya . . ." He said a bunch of other things about morels but I wasn't listening. Gracious and I had been going after morels in the spring since I was in first grade. We halved them and dried them in the sun, later hanging them on strings in the basement. When Gracious wanted some to roll in flour and fry with butter, I'd go down in the basement and bring them up and set them in a pan of water to plump up.

At the turn-around point, we took our first real break and lolled around a stand of black oak drinking water from our canteens and eating cheese and lunchmeat sandwiches.

"Christ," Poteet said scornfully as Nick and Irwin left the trail and went off westward into the woods as the rest of us started on our candy bars. "What a chickenshit outfit this is . . . say, your mom coming over tonight, Larry?" There was something like eagerness in his voice.

"Uh, yeah . . . I think so, far's I know," I said, knowing nothing could stop Gracious from being there. "How 'bout you, your folks coming?"

"Well, it'd just be my dad . . . if he comes . . ." His face fell.

"He probably will," I said heartily.

"Think so?" Poteet said, but letting no hope penetrate his sudden gloom.

"Sure, he'll want to watch you show those other assholes how it's done in the canoe race."

I wandered around, looking for more shrunken morels but couldn't find any.

Nick and Irwin came back, Nick leading the way. They were both angry and flushed, and a silvery strand of saliva hung down from Nick's left ear. "Well, guys! No more goddamn mushrooms anywhere, whattaya say we saddle up," Nick said heartily, falsely, brushing pine needles off his left shoulder. "C'mon, no kidding, let's get this shithook operation on the road, I got things to do back at camp . . ."

There was a wet spot on the ass of his shorts about the size of a saucer.

Irwin was bright red and he was careful not to meet anyone's eyes. There were twigs in his brush cut and a bright red scratch across his right cheek.

On the trip back, Poteet and I fell back until the others were about ten yards ahead. Poteet glanced over at me. "You see the signs of Nick and Irwin playing grab-ass in the woods? Man, I can't stand that little fucker Irwin. If it wasn't a mismatch, I think I'd kick the shit out of him just for fun."

"Hey, you got my permission, Jim."

A smile split Poteet's face, wide and happy, the first such I'd seen on him. I wondered why everyone called him Jim to his face and Poteet in his absence.

"Well, tellya, Larry, an opportunity for something almost as good turned up the other day . . ."

"Yeah?"

"Yeah."

"Well, I don't like the prick either. Whadja do?"

"Well, on our last hike we took this break, see, and ole Irwin slips off very quietly into the woods. Well, I'd discovered the bastard's got bashful kidneys, so when I see him heading out for a nice private piss, I follow him, see, ole Injun Jim, not making a sound like a true Scout . . . I slip behind a tree when he turns and looks to be sure he's alone, then, soon's I hear his little tinkle on the leaves, I step right up beside him: 'Hey, there, Irwin, great place for a nice, refreshing piss, eh?' And I haul out right next to 'im—our shoulders were almost touching—and I tell you, buddy, I loosed a stream a draft horse woulda been proud of. Naturally *his* stream dried up the instant he saw me, and he's frozen there like a jack-lighted deer with his little white willy in his hand. Well, when I'm somewhere near the end, well, you see, for some unknown reason he's wearing his Scout shoes all polished up, and I can't resist, I give both his feet a good hosing, got his socks pretty good too, then I tell 'im, 'Oh gosh, oh golly, I'm just so sorry there, Irwin, sir, didn't mean to piss on you like that, but don't worry about it, piss's mostly just sterile water anyhow. Well, gotta go, seeya around . . .'"

Jim's eyes gleamed with reminiscence and I couldn't stop wild laughter from burbling up from deep inside me until I was gasping and can hardly see. Through tear-swept eyes I saw Poteet grinning, looking very, very pleased with himself.

For Waterfront Night more cars appeared than on the Sunday we'd arrived. Things looked promising and everyone seemed in a festive mood as shadows began to lengthen and the mostly pastel car bodies began to be stippled with dew.

"Hi . . . Hi . . ." people called out and were greeted in return: "Hi . . . Hi . . ."

There were two charcoal grills made from oil drums cut in half, then mounted horizontally on cast iron legs. Curly's friend Jerry from the kitchen stood behind a long buffet table laden with burgers, hot dogs, baked beans, potato salad, chips, tossed salad, brownies, and various condiments, serving people from the grills and occasionally returning to the Lodge to resupply.

Scouts not competing in any of the waterfront events mostly wore full uniforms, most with long trousers, as they filed before the buffet table, stoking plates with hot dogs, hamburgers, potato salad, baked beans. There were plenty of Coke bottles in big aluminum pots from the kitchen filled with water and ice.

Gracious pulled in and the Chevy disappeared from sight between two larger cars. I wondered if Alex Fuller had come with her as he'd promised earlier. Yes: now that I'd moved closer, I could see someone was in the passenger seat . . . and someone was in the rear seat as well. God almighty, it was Deanna, whose russet hair caught a bit of retreating sun. I could feel my face brighten, my heart speed up, my breathing go a bit ragged.

Curly and I stood together as the three, spying me, approached us. We both wore khaki shorts, T-shirts, and tennis shoes—I'd go back to the tent and put my suit on under my shorts in a little while so I could just slip out of my clothes when it got to be time for the 100-meter race.

Gracious couldn't help herself and stepped forward, pulled me to her, and gave me a brief hug, then stepped back quickly to survey me. She wore her Kappa Kappa Gamma pin on the wide lapel of a dark blue dress with white trim.

"Oh, my, Larry, you look just *splendid*, really in the pink, you must be having *such* a wonderful time. Since Alex was going to come with me I thought it'd be nice to ask Anna too, aren't you glad? Anna, have you ever been over here before?"

"Don't think so, Missus Carstairs." She came slowly over to stand beside Gracious. She wore tight faded jeans, and again I thought of the time I'd gone over to the Fullers earlier in the summer to see Alex and had found Deanna sitting under the huge mulberry tree in the Fuller backyard in a half-full washtub of warm water in her black tank suit, but also wearing a new pair of Levi's—the idea was to make them conform and cling to her shape when they dried.

Later, when I saw them swaying in the breeze on the Fuller clothesline, my mouth went dry. It felt kind of dry right now too.

"How do you do, Mrs. Carstairs," Curly said smoothly, extending his hand, smiling. "I'm Larry's tent-mate, Curly Norrys . . . and I'm glad I am, 'cause we've discovered we've got a lot of things in common, right, Larry?"

"That we do," I said, sneaking another look at Deanna. As a little girl her hair had been new-penny bright, but now that she was fourteen it had darkened. She often wore it in two thick braids, as she did this evening, and the lowering red sun gave it the hue of dried blood. These days she liked to call it auburn.

". . . Deanna Fuller," Gracious was saying, "and her brother and Larry's good friend, Alex."

"Hiya," Alex muttered. He was seventeen, about my height, but was heavier and much stronger. His hair was black and wavy and he had long sideburns. Already he shaved about once a week. I liked the way he was kind of wild and always testing adult authority. He was probably as good a friend as I had.

"Hiya!" Curly stuck his hand out first to Deanna who, surprised, took it, looking at him in wonder. I doubted she'd ever had her hand shaken thus by a male. Then Curly extended his hand to Alex, and I wondered again about his fondness for shaking hands at every occasion. "Hey, you wanta take a look around, Alex? Want me to showya some of the sights of this noble institution?"

"Uh, sure," Alex said. He was sizing up Curly, and like others seemed to be instantly intrigued by him. I wasn't surprised—somehow I'd known Curly and Alex would hit it off.

As they moved off in the direction of the waterfront, I heard Alex say, "Wow, sure looks like lottsa stuff to do around here . . ."

"Aw, not so much as you'd think," Curly said in a low voice. "But you can always think up something." They looked and sounded like old pals of years' standing.

"Must be tough with no girls."

"Yeah. That's mostly what's the matter with this place," Curly said. "That's what the lifeguards say too."

Curly and Alex drifted off together without a backward glance, heading down toward the waterfront, and I wondered if Curly maybe had some more beer stashed down there somewhere.

"My," Gracious said, "I do believe I'm in need of a little nourishment . . . I think I'll just go have a little of that potato salad . . . it looks *awfully* good, and maybe just a few baked beans . . . I don't suppose you'll eat anything, Larry, until after you've swum . . ."

"Right."

I was startled to find Deanna at my side, her bare arm almost touching my own. "Where you going, Larry?"

"Back to my tent, gotta put my bathing suit on—I'm gonna swim in the 100-meter race in a little while."

"Good, I'll come along and keep you company. I'm not all that hungry anyhow, though everything does look pretty good . . ."

As we walked the trail toward my and Curly's tent, Anna suddenly reached out and took my hand, just as if we were an adult couple, and we walked along, swinging our clasped hands between us. Hers was damp and her fingers felt strong as she intertwined them with mine.

At my tent, I went in while Anna looked doubtfully into the dark interior through the half-drawn-back flaps and wrinkled her nose—maybe the smell of wet bathing suits and sodden towels. I went in and shut the flaps. I was about to drop my shorts and put on my bathing suit when I heard her put a foot on the step—and on entering, catch the toe of her left Keds on one of Curly's hiking boots, which I'd not noticed had been dead center in the entrance, and she tripped, falling forward so that I had to catch her in my arms, just as they did in movies. Her arms came around behind my back and she pressed against me and somehow or other we ended up kissing, our arms tightly fastened around each other—no, not just kissing, not the silly stuff they called "smooching" in eighth grade: for I briefly felt the tip of her tongue in my mouth. This had never happened to me before, and I suddenly felt as if I'd never been more alive. And also as if I were in danger of fainting.

This was clearly something like Messing Around, as the high school kids said. I felt a sudden crazy pang of fear at the thought of starting high school in the coming fall.

"Well, I guess we're prob'ly missing the cookout. Prob'ly we oughta get back there . . ." Deanna murmured in my ear. I could almost fill in her thoughts: *Before they wonder where we are and what we might be up to . . .*

"Well, hmm, yeah, here, why don't you step outside and I'll put my trunks on under my shorts and we can go back."

"Okay." And she stepped out.

It was a good thing she went when she did because I was having a hard time concealing my boner . . . if I'd had the time and privacy I'd probably have choked my chicken on the spot.

As it was, I crammed my swollen cock into my jock and pulled on my nylon trunks.

And then I found and pulled on a huge oyster-colored sweat-shirt whose hem fell almost to my knees. I decided not to mess with putting my shorts back on over my swimsuit. Why bother?

Back at the buffet area, we found Curly chatting animatedly with Gracious, responding to her like certain of the high school guys did, especially the brains and bookworms who wanted to go to college and so took her as their guide, trusted her, believed in her problem-solving abilities, her will to do something helpful for each of them. And each came from a family where the mother always played second banana to an I-run-the-show husband.

I didn't see Alex anywhere.

"Really, Missus Carstairs," Curly was saying, "keep your eye on Larry in the 100-meter freestyle swim . . . he's really fast, I think he's gonna win . . ."

Deanna and I were just back in time to see the canoe race start: six guys in swimming trunks, including Irwin and Poteet, each with a paddleless canoe, shoved off from the shallows just offshore, and quickly jumped up so their feet were planted on the gunwales on either side of the stern—then they began pumping up and down as savagely as they could without losing their balance, looking a bit like mantises as they propelled themselves forward. They managed to pass behind a buoy about two minutes later, then headed back for the beach, pumping with everything they had. No one fell, though Irwin looked pretty shaky at times.

Poteet won!—and he had the perfect look of a winner, his face split in a huge grin, his mesomorph's physique twitching like a living anatomy chart, his eyes scanning the crowd . . . and scanning again, after which his face fell and took on a look of something like sorrow, and in less than a minute he walked away, slinging a towel over his shoulder, stuffing his blue ribbon into a pocket of his swimsuit.

There was no line now at the buffet table so Deanna and I went over and got paper plates, but while Anna loaded her plate, I picked up a couple stalks of celery filled with Cheez Whiz and nibbled on them since I'd be competing in minutes. They seemed awfully salty and I kept swallowing over and over.

Anna's hand brushed mine and I almost jerked it away, fearful someone might see. When I looked over at her, her dark blue gaze was upon me and it didn't look admiring. I could feel my cheeks redden. For the first time in a while, I dropped my gaze before another's. I slipped off my oversized sweatshirt and held it out to Anna, looking up again: "Could you hang onto me . . . I mean hang onto this thing until I get back?"

"Sure." She smiled.

Bart was at the shore by the dock, and my four competitors had gathered by him. ". . . So be sure we see one hand whack one of the buoys on that line fifty meters out, fellas, then turn around however you like—the first to get back to the starting buoy at dock's end wins . . ."

Bud wasn't here—maybe he was off with "my baby!" somewhere far away from the lights and the shouting here, maybe parked on some quiet back road where, gazing at the splinter of moon, they might have some privacy.

I must have stored some energy up because as soon as I am stroking with the others toward the distant bobbing line of buoys, I feel myself getting stronger, faster, and since there's nobody in front the others must be behind: I pour it on, hand over hand, turning my head up every three strokes so I can keep an eye on the approaching line of buoys—

—*Smack* goes my right hand loudly on a bobbing buoy, I turn quickly and begin pulling toward shore—I'm even faster than on the way out, and since I know where I'm going I don't bother to keep an eye on the shore—have I ever swum faster or with more intensity?

I feel the water warming, know I must be near shore, and lift my head to see how close I am: Christ almighty, the dock is not directly before me, it is far, far to my right!

So now instead of being the plucky underdog winning the race, I'm the fool who forget to look where he was going and ended up in the shallows fifty feet from where Irwin was being handed the blue ribbon. I wasn't even placing second or third out of five, I was dead last. Dan Denton, a kid who was sometimes taken for me and I for him so much did we resemble each other, was second, Kyle Riker third, and Bob-something fourth.

I seemed to move more and more slowly as I approached the dock and the chattering winners. I could see Deanna and Gracious watching me from the corner of my eye. Andy was standing beside them, smiling. I trudged on toward them.

In minutes, Bart set off a small fireworks display from the end of the dock and a few rockets sputtered off into the air, to explode in dazzling circles of white and purple sparks that then drifted down lazily upon the water.

By around 9:30 people began to get ready to leave, so before things got too far underway, Perky took the microphone set up on the dock and without any preamble sang to the audience in his deep resonant voice:

> *"Good night, ladies, good night, gents . . .*
> *Good night, ladies, we're going to leave you now . . .*
> *Hope you had a happy time, happy time, happy time,*
> *Hope you had a happy time,*
> *We had a good time too . . ."*

"Oh, that was just lovely," Gracious said, "just like you might hear on Lawrence Welk. Well, Larry and Andy, you'll surely see me somewhere along East Front Street on Saturday, during the Cherry Festival parade—I'll be somewhere among the crowd with my trusty Kodak, filming it."

Alex came sauntering up from the direction of the Lodge, chewing gum savagely. Andy and I looked at each other and he smiled—he had been very glad to see Gracious, his favorite teacher.

Deanna sat demurely in the back seat—Alex always liked to ride shotgun—and she tucked her legs up under her bottom.

When she looked at me after a few moments of looking anywhere but in my direction, I was startled: expecting a pleasant ordinary smile, she favored me instead with a look of dark uncertainty and intensity that deepened the ordinary blue of her eyes to the dark blue of Grand Traverse Bay when there's plenty of light but little sun. "Here, Larry." She extended her hand and I took from her fingers a roll of cherry Life Savers with a single blossom of Indian paintbrush Scotch-taped to it. The rims of her ears reddened.

"Thanks."

I felt an impulse to touch Deanna on her shoulder, but stopped myself quickly.

She looked sharply up at me: "It was nice seeing you again, Larry," she said, as if I'd just returned from a long journey.

"Same here. Thanks for coming." I didn't want to say anything to Gracious since I still called her "Mamma," and thought it was too kid stuff. "Thanks for all three of you guys for coming—sorry I messed up the race. Guess I learned something the hard way. Again."

Gracious and Anna rolled their eyes, fluttered their hands, to show how absurd such an apology was. Alex was smirking and his eyes were bright; he was chewing gum savagely, so I guessed he and Curly had snuck off for beer during the entertainment. When I got back home I'd have to ask Alex what he thought of Curly.

Gracious called to me just before she put the Chevy in gear: "Be sure to invite Curly to come see us sometime after camp's over, Larry . . . he's certainly awfully sophisticated for fourteen. Well, see you at the parade on Saturday. Say goodbye to Andy for me . . ."

"Sure thing."

I'd only been in my sleeping bag for about fifteen minutes and wasn't asleep when Curly came in. I'd been trying to get rid of my boner by keeping my thoughts off Deanna, and had almost nodded off.

I could smell the beer as soon as he came through the flap in spite of the Spearmint he was chewing.

He kicked off his moccasins and got into his sleeping bag without getting undressed and began talking almost immediately about queers again, though this yarn was different from the others.

". . . Well, I'll tell you how, Larry, though it's my guess and somebody else might come up with something else . . . ya know, my old man used to warn me about queers every time before I went back to boarding school. He told me it was possible to turn queer overnight too, if you spent much time in their company or thinking about it, and that scared the living shit out of me, I can tell you . . . but what really did its work was the old man himself, y'see, Larry, when I was twelve . . . on the eve of leaving for Switzerland my old man came into my room where I was sleeping . . . I felt him get in bed with me and I could feel he was naked, and he was pressing up against my back and he had a gigantic boner and was pressing it against my ass . . . and it was *big*, man, my old man's hung like a horse, I mean a real schlong, y'know? I was scared shitless and when I tried to scrooch away from him, he put his big heavy arm around me and held me still . . . I could feel his dick sliding up and down the crack in my ass, looking for the hole, and so I shrieked out! '*Goddamn you!*' I screamed. 'You fuckin' queer, get *offa* me, get outta my goddamn bed!'

"Well, he does, and he has this funny glazed look in his eyes and slowly they come back to looking like who I thought he was, and he looks around and says, 'What the hell? What's going on here?'

"Here's the thing, Larry . . . he tells me he'd taken a snootful of medication with wine and what he was doing was done when he was *sleepwalking*, if you can feature that!

"So here's what I don't know, Larry: was it like he said, he was in this kinda trance . . . or did he just fake it? Ambiguity, Larry, that's the river that runs through my life . . . sometimes it's like I can't tell what anything *really* is . . . whether things'r off or on . . . in or out, is something gray more black than it is white? Or black? . . . always something keeping me from *knowing* for sure what's *really* happening, so that's why I kinda push people sometimes, it's to find out, you know, like what's what, so they reveal who they really are and then I know . . . I gotta lure the real person out like you do when you're fishing, y'know? . . . say, do you believe in God, Larry?"

"No."

"Wow! That's great! Neither do I. Never for an instant! But ya better watch out, saying you're an atheist is like saying you're an insane killer or something, talk about being ostracized, shit, an atheist couldn't even get a job as shoveler at the shitworks . . . can I ask ya, how come you don't?"

"Well, dunno exactly . . . maybe it's just that all that stuff just never took, never stuck . . . you know, the water-into-wine stuff . . . virgin birth, raising the dead, casting out demons . . . the Ascension . . . guess I just don't—can't—believe in that kinda supernatural stuff . . ."

"*Wow!* Me too, Larry! Me too!"

Six

On Thursday morning Curly, Andy, Steve Crawley (Ned Fangbone had suddenly taken to making himself scarce), and Dick Bentley and some other guy from another pod—maybe it was Hank Esperanza—were doing another hike, probably the last of the week. They'd asked me but I lied, telling them I'd promised Bart I'd be around the waterfront if he needed me for anything. I'd been around too many people for a while, and it'd be good to hang around the waterfront with hardly anybody around and life flowing so slowly you could relax, stretch, feel the sun, and breathe easy.

I left our pod around nine—why bother with breakfast—and when I was about halfway to the waterfront Poteet stepped like some kind of Indian from behind a massive oak. I'd almost forgotten he existed and I must have jumped a little.

"Hey, easy-steady there, big fella," Poteet said, scowling first, then grinning. "It's just me. Merely me." He wore trunks and had a towel over one burly shoulder.

"Jim, how's she going?"

"Okay, I guess. Headin' for the waterfront?"

"Yeah."

"How's about I tag along? I didn't want to do another goddamn hike or fuck around with bows and arrows. And those pissy single-shot .22s. Christ, .22 shorts are chickenshit ammo. Thought maybe I c'd just kinda bum around the waterfront . . . tireda Curly and the rest too . . . I been here once before and I tellya, it wears pretty thin pretty fast."

I felt like telling him that was just about how I felt but didn't. "Hey, those waterfront guys know you're my friend, right, so they'll probably let me stay and maybe cop a swim and fart around?"

"Uh, yeah, think so . . . best to ask Bart and tell'im you'll be happy to run errands or anything . . . yeah, he knows you're from my pod, should be no sweat." It occurred to me that even though everything seemed okay this time around at Camp G, it somehow wasn't nearly as much fun as last year had been—maybe all that yakking about queers was messing things up. Or maybe we all needed a little more direction.

"Sure thing."

We walked along slowly. It was a nice day, with the heat mellowed by a variety of breezes. My feet were bare, but their soles were tough enough by now so the gravel didn't bother them.

As we passed by, a blue jay on a hemlock exchanged an angry look with me. Its eye was bright on me as it appeared to whet its beak on a branch. I could hear some droning insects from time to time.

"Boy," Poteet said, "y'know, you guys don't know just how good you have it."

"Huh?"

"I mean Jesus, look here, you and Curly and Andy all had at least onea your folks come over for Waterfront Night—me, my old man promised, but naturally the bastard didn't follow through. He hardly ever does." Poteet was squeezing and relaxing his hands and his forearm muscles writhed like snakes.

I was astonished: "Curly and Andy's folks were here last night?"

"Well, yeah, Andy's mother and Curly's father were both here . . . Andy's two kinda hefty sisters were there too . . ."

"Wow, no shit, Vera and June too, eh? No, well, I didn't see either one I guess . . ." I'd only briefly glimpsed Andy on Waterfront Night and I sure hadn't seen his mother, Ruth Dellums—too bad,

I liked her, and she and Gracious were friends. "What was Curly's dad like?"

"Well, you'd remember this guy if you saw him—just about the total fucking opposite of Curly: he's this kinda short dark kinda guy, everything about him looks kinda *thick,* you know? His hands. His neck. Hadda a real heada black oily-looking hair. Hadda real five o'clock shadow, this black silk suit with no cuffs on his pants and these kinda pointy-toed shoes? Hadda big gold wristwatch and cufflinks and coupla big gold rings? Tell you, Larry, he looked kinda like something out of a goddamn gangster movie—sorta like Edward G. Robinson in *Key Largo.* Y'ever see that?"

"Yeah, uh, thought it was pretty good—saw it at the Ermine Falls free show last summer . . . and yeah, now that you mention it, I think I *did* get a glimpse of that guy . . ."

In fact, I'd seen such a guy engaged in conversation with Perky: thickness, Poteet's word, came pretty close, and it was hard to believe tall thin blond live-wire Curly could have come from his dick.

We reached the waterfront. Bart was in the near tower and when he stood up from his corner seat, I could see he was clutching a *Saturday Evening Post.* He looked bored, but he brightened when he saw Poteet and me. When he put the magazine on the rail around the tower, I could see the illustration of a young man and a woman, holding hands and walking by a seashore.

"Guys," he called down. "Good to see you. Look around, we're damn near deserted here. Pretty peaceful, huh?"

A couple of younger Scouts were paddling around aimlessly in the beginner area on paddle-boards. I could see two canoes out on the lake, each with two guys.

"Where's Bud?" I asked.

"Where'd you be if you had this gorgeous girl in a gorgeous car and she wanted to tear you away from this paradise for a little while and go somewhere where you might just find a little privacy?" His voice sounded envious—and why not, who wouldn't envy Bud? I recalled the woman's fair hair, her smooth skin . . . but then her image faded and Deanna's took its place, grinning.

"I think I can answer *that* one pretty damn quick," Poteet said.

"Yeah," I said, but couldn't think of anything else to say.

I thought how in a way I hadn't been all that thrilled to see Deanna arrive the other night but after she was gone I felt, for the first time, her absence, and felt as if I should have said something more to her—but what?

Of course Bart had no objection to our swimming. We both switched our tags from Inactive to Active on the swim board and went out on the dock. Poteet dove in and did a showy overhand out to the bobbing diving raft, came back, toweled off and left, smiling and giving me a wink, as if he'd accomplished something; likely he'd just wanted to be around somebody friendly and be included in things for a little while. If he liked you, he was really a friendly guy.

I wondered why Curly hadn't brought his father around and introduced him—Gracious would no doubt have gotten a kick out of him—she tended to like people who were a little out-of-round, she'd have gotten the bugger locked into a chat and would have figured him out, pronto; and I'd've liked to've looked him over, him who'd maybe been (or maybe not) sleepwalking when he'd maybe tried (or maybe not) to queer his son. Unless of course Curly'd made the entire thing up.

"Hey, Larry." It was Bart. I'd been so lost in thought I'd almost forgotten where I was and what I was doing: standing dumbly on the dock, looking into the water. "Y'know, I bet we could polish off those last two items for your Lifesaving merit badge in about ten minutes, if you want to. He had a current *Handbook For Boys* and was looking into it. "Numbers eight and nine read, 'Surface dive in six to eight feet, recovering various objects three times and a ten-pound weight once,' and then, 'In deep water, remove street clothes,' there's an asterisk, and 'swim 100 yards.' The asterisked part says, 'means socks, low shoes, underwear (or bathing suit), trousers, shirt, tie and coat, or sweater or sweatshirt.' Well, hell, no reason to screw around with the clothes stuff, and let's not mess around with that 'various objects' bullshit. But why don't you get our diving stones, and if you bring'em up according to the book and I'll sign for both items . . ."

"Geeze, that'd be great, Bart. Thanks."

I lie floating on my back, watching Bart approach, carrying a round rock with "10#" painted on it with silver paint. Another that reads "15#" rests at his feet.

I clear my lungs and duck my head a couple of times as Bart swings the silvered rock back, then swings it forward and releases it: it goes up in a gentle parabola, and before it comes down, I aim my arms straight ahead, turn upside down, and swim for the bottom. *Fooom!* goes the stone and I can see it wobbling down toward the tan corrugated bottom, a comet's tail of silver bubbles following it. When the stone hits the sand, a cloud arises, momentarily obscuring it.

I reach it easily and go to pick it up, knowing it should be easy enough in the water, but it's a slippery son of a bitch and I can't seem to get a good grip on it: every time I try, it slips and slides like I'm going to lose it. I'm running out of air. But finally I get both hands on it and hold it like I'm about to shoot an underhand free throw, my feet planted on sand that feels like it's sucking me down. I lower to a squat, then drive upward for a start, but kicking furiously only gets me up to within a few feet of the surface and I can't seem to make any forward movement, plus I'm running out of air. I'll have to drop the fucker, surface, and go back . . . when I think of Curly and for some reason that brings new power to my legs and I'm able to thrash my way to the surface and hold onto the dock with one hand and muscle the rock onto it with my other. I'm gasping.

"Whew," Bart says, "damn, I'm worn out for you, Larry. But hey, congrats, that does the trick, your ticket'll be officially punched, kiddo . . . and by the way, that was the fifteen-pound rock . . . I knew you could do it."

"Thanks" is all I can get out. I face the dock, put my hands on it, kick up out of the water until my arms are straight, then spin my ass around so it smacks down on the water-drenched boards. I'm trembling, but not from cold or exertion—I was shocked that Bart had played what I guess was a kind of practical joke on me . . . but what if I hadn't been able to do it? My wind is returning and my heart throttles down. I feel a little exhilarated because I could get the rock up and onto the dock; maybe Bart hadn't pulled a fast one on me but wanted me to show myself I could do it.

I was about ready to leave and had my towel over my shoulder and was headed for the tag board to check myself out. And here came Andy, all by himself, trudging along, his towel clutched in one hand, dragging on the ground.

"Hiya, Andy!" I greeted him. "Great morning for a dip, huh? Especially for someone who's a Swimmer."

"You bet. Guess you already been in, huh?" He looked disappointed.

"Yeah, I just finished up something with Bart on my Lifesaving merit badge. But another dip sounds good about now, whaddaya say we haul out to the diving raft and dry out in the sun?"

"Sure thing, that'd be great, uh, and I, uh, wanted to ask you about something anyhow, Larry . . ."

We go out and to the raft and float around and dive and futz around in general. After a time, we get back up on the diving raft, a wooden platform over six empty fifty-five-gallon drums, and sit on its perimeter, looking into the water, letting the sun dry us. The chop lifts the raft gently up and down. We can barely see the bottom, where currents have made whorls in the darkish sand. The barrels sometimes make a clunking sound.

"Yup, this's a real nice day, huh?" I say, lying back on the warm boards, shielding my eyes from the sun with my forearm. "Hardly a cloud in the sky except for those thunderheads to the east . . ."

"Yeah. Pretty nice . . . say, Larry, how can you tell if you're queer or not?"

I sit up, wipe my face with my towel. "Jesus . . . what's the deal, Andy, Curly ragging you about that shit? Man, that guy's got queers on the brain, though I don't know exactly why . . ." I think about saying, Y'know, maybe he's queer himself.

Why ask me? Because Andy was so in awe of my mother and so trusted her it wouldn't have occurred to him that maybe I wasn't cut from the same trustworthy and level-headed cloth as she was, though it was hard to imagine him asking Gracious what he'd just asked me.

"Oh, no, it's just I think he's maybe suspicious."

"Suspicious? God, he's got a lotta nerve. Of what?"

"Me. I think maybe Curly thinks I'm queer."

I don't know what to say. "Why?"

"I dunno exactly—maybe 'cause I want to be an actor, 'cause I can sing and dance and play the piano and everybody seems to think people like that're just about all queer—'course lots of them I guess are . . . and 'course I'm not one of those athletic types like Jim . . . but I don't think I look like a queer . . . do I, Larry?"

"Christ almighty, Andy, whaddaya . . . whaddaya think your average queer is supposed to look like anyhow?"

"Oh, I dunno, you know, uh, flitty and girly-like or something . . . kinda high voices and a little wiggle when they walk . . . I hear some wear eyeliner and even lipstick. But I mean, how canya sure-fire tell, deep down, if ya are or might be queer? Curly says it's possible you can turn into one overnight."

His look is so pained and his cherub's face so bright red and earnest I almost like him. He looks like he might be on the verge of throwing up, or rolling off the raft and sinking as fast as that fifteen-pound rock to the bottom of Lake Greavey.

"Well," I say, trying to sound as thoughtful as Gracious, all the time wondering how she'd handle this. "Well, y'know, somebody asked me that not too long ago, and I'll tellya what I told him: what you do is, see, y'ask yourself this: would you ever *really* want to do any of that stuff queers are known for? You know, the main stuff is like blowjobs and cornholing, all the rest is some kinda variation on those items—so, does that excite ya or give ya the creeps? And another thing to ask yourself is, do you really like girls? Like, does the thought of feeling one up get you excited? Well, if it's No for the first and Yes for the second, then it's for damn sure you're no queer, Andy . . ."

Andy remains deep in thought for long seconds as he thinks it over. "Well," he finally says, looking up, his eyes abrim with gratitude, "you know when I did see Deanna again at Waterfront Night, I thought how cute she was and how she was maybe the kinda girl I might like to start going around with, you know, and maybe take to movies and stuff . . . when she was here I could see her little nippy-nips poking out against her shirt and that . . . gave me a funny kinda feeling." His eyes are a little filmed over and I see he's still examining his image of Deanna.

"You'd make a nice couple," I say through my teeth. Nippy-nips! for Christ's sake. Something about the term is giving me a boner and pissing me off at the same time. Nippy-nips. The little son of a bitch.

"Hey, Larry . . . c'n I ask you something else?"

"Sure."

"You think Curly'll think I'm dumb if I . . . well, when I get back home, I think maybe I'm gonna start using 'Drew' for my first name—do you think it's a dumb idea?"

I hesitated, then decided to bolster him: "Nah, hell, anyone should be able to call himself what he wants. Drew sounds like a good name for somebody who's gonna be a performer . . ."

He looks relieved and I almost wince at his trusting look. "Thanks, Larry."

"Let's go," I say, brushing dried sand off my belly. "You're fine, Andy, perfectly fine . . ."

We were about halfway to the Lodge when we heard running feet behind us and we both turned: quickly catching us with his huge athletic strides came Poteet, his yellow nylon trunks covered with brown eels flapping against his powerful thighs.

We walked back to the pod together to change for lunch.

Curly was in the tent when I went in, lying on his back, hands behind his head, staring up into the canvassy gloom.

"How's it goin', Curly? What's up?"

"Oh, well, not so hot, I'm tryinna find this lady undertaker I heard about—see, I gotta stiff I wanta bury—argh, ach du lieber, in der bed I haff gee-shitten . . . that's German in case ya don't know . . ."

"Hey, Poteet was telling me your old man came to Waterfront Night after all."

"Yeah, yeah, he was there all right . . . pity you missed ole Vartan, though, Larry, I'd've been happy to introduce you . . ."

"Vartan?"

"Yeah . . . old Fartin' Vartan . . . y'know Larry, how there's these different kindsa farts? A phuz. A phiz? A phiz-phuzz, a tear-ass, a rattler, a blart . . . and the famous SBD, the silent-but-deadly? Lemme tellya, Vartan can blow an egg fart that has a little of all those others in it . . . ah, the piquancy, the pungency, the range . . . his beer farts'll eat the paint offa your car . . ." There were almost tears in his eyes.

"Think maybe I saw him from a distance," I said cautiously.

"You *did*? How'd you know it was him?" His eyes were suddenly bright as a squirrel's.

"Poteet kinda described him to me this morning . . ."

"What'd the fucker say, huh, that Vartan looked like some kinda greaser?"

"Christ, no! He said your old man looked solid and wealthy and maybe kinda . . . well, European."

"Well, he got that part right," Curly said sulkily. "So what else did Poteet have to say about 'im?"

At dinner that night our pod reassembled as usual, taking our usual table, keeping the usual spare seats on either side of us. Curly seemed preoccupied: occasionally he and Andy would each casually shoot a glance at the other, then quickly lower their gazes. Ned Fangbone and Steve Crawley turned up together for the first time in a while and both dug into their Swiss steaks with a vengeance and without looking up—oddly, none of the rest of us seemed to have much appetite.

So what was the deal with Curly and Andy? Was Curly really warming up to Andy and actually liking him? Was he setting him up to shoot him down because he thought Andy was queer? Or was Curly himself queer and intent upon turning Andy into one if he wasn't one already? Or something else altogether?

After the dining hall had been cleared and the few used tables given a hasty wipe with a damp dishtowel by a sweating Jerry Bronson, Perky stood up at his front-row-center table, the only one there save two Scouts from Leelanau, the round-faced Ed Cookie and his pal Skinny Ted Cruickshank.

Perky made ding-a-ling sounds with his spoon on a glass, and conversations halted. He rose and cleared his throat.

I'd thought maybe there wasn't going to be any presentation tonight but was glad I was wrong. Anything Perky did seemed something worth paying attention to.

"Lads," Perky began, "I'd hoped that tonight's, um, entertainment was going to be one of my favorite films of Harold Lloyd, whose humor I thought might offer a smallish antidote to the cruelty and mindless nihilistic buffoonery of morons like the Three Stooges, whose work I wouldn't deign to even call slapstick, oh, but it's *something* on a stick all right, if you get my drift . . ."

My head jerked up: My God, Perky'd really said, hadn't he, if you puzzled out his sentence, that the Stooges were, in his opinion, "Shit on a stick!"

Nobody but me seemed to catch on, not even Curly who was frowning at Andy, whose eyes were fixed on Perky.

Every time I learned something new about Perky, the better I liked him.

"However, fellas, that was impossible, never mind why, so I thought I'd run a couple of short silent black-and-white cartoons from the previous decade, during which, as you know, one of the momentous events in our country's history occurred, gentlemen, namely World War Two—there may be no such thing as a good war, but I believe it's possible for there to be a just war, and also a war of necessity. What have these cartoons have to do with the war? Perhaps not much on first blush. But as Krazy Kat will demonstrate, some of those particularly and even peculiarly American inner resources and attributes that helped us win that war will be on display: perseverance, steadfastness, creativity, improvisation,

and optimism, among other things, we'll leave patriotism for another time . . . well, let's take a look at these two items . . ."

And on came the creaking black-and-white film, so remote
from the workings of Camp G it seemed we might be viewing
life on another planet: a heavily lipsticked would-be dancer with
blonde corkscrew curls and huge black shoes, bearing her drama
school diploma, sneaks into a chorus girl rehearsal, beseeches the
self-important director, angry Krazy Kat, to give her an audition;
to get his attention otherwise, she looses her singing voice, which
electrifies all the chorus girls . . . so of course she becomes the star of
the production—"Christ's teeth, Busby Berkeley writ small," Curly
muttered in my ear. In the final production, she and Krazy Kat kiss
as the circle of light enclosing them gets smaller and smaller until
the screen goes black. The lights came on.

I was eager to hear Perky's commentary, but he said nothing as
he rewound the film and threaded another into the projector. He
called for lights to be doused: this time wartime aviator Mickey
Mouse is fighting a Nazi-like Black Pete: Mickey and Black Pete
fight an air battle in which Mickey's plane is damaged in various
ways but he always improvises repairs on the fly. In the final se-
quence, Mickey swoops the nose of his propeller-less plane into a
windmill and its blades become his new propeller; Mickey's plane
is harpooned from behind by Black Pete in his villainous black
aircraft, so Mickey gets tough and dives down close to the ground,
dragging Pete through a bell tower, a cactus patch, and finally, when
Mickey successfully lands, two dog policemen are waiting for Black
Pete with a big bag and they capture him as he comes rolling up to
them. After the bag is cinched tightly around Black Pete's throat,
Mickey clasps his white-gloved hands—or paws?—overhead and
accepts victory. He's joined atop his ruined plane by Minnie, who
smooches him as the various animals of the audience go nuts, jumping up and down in joy and celebration.

"In addition to those qualities I noted with the first film as exempla-
ry aspects of our national character," Perky intones in his mellowest
voice at the film's end, not yet letting the lights be turned back on,

"I feel there are others we can add after seeing Mickey vanquish the fascistic Black Pete—I'm sure you've remarked his Nazi-ish aspect. But think too of those qualities exemplified by our side, pluckiness, following through, inventiveness, and especially improvisation, not to mention a sound grasp of the obvious, and the grit to deal with tough situations when it's required. It's what comes with knowing when to walk and when to run and when to hold your ground."

As I was thinking Perky's words over, Curly abruptly stood and using the gloom as a cloak, slipped out through the front door just as Perky had the lights put on. I'd been planning on asking Curly what "knee-a-listick" was.

Afterward, I went down to the waterfront, but it was pretty much deserted. A light was on in the guardshack and two on the dock, but I didn't check to see if anyone was there.

I didn't find Curly after a five-minute hike to the archery range either, so I went back to our tent. I used my L-headed Scout flashlight as I straightened up my bunk and stretched out on my cot in my skivvies, propping my neck and head against my rolled sleeping bag. It felt good to close my eyes and stop thinking.

I heard Poteet approaching—by now I recognized his firm machine-like tread—and he stopped before my tent, then pulled the flap back and shot his flashlight's beam around: "Where the fuck is everybody, Larry? Hey, it's darker'n a well-digger's ass in here. Christ, even Nick and Irwin are gone somewhere, but who gives a shit about those two pricks. Anyhow, I can't find Curly or Andy or even those other two dumb Tenderfoot shits whose names I can't remember, you know, Acey and Deucey there. Fric'n Frac. Christ, what's going on?"

"Damn if I know—I was just wondering that myself."

We talked a little of Perky's goofy presentation—hearing all that serious stuff that was supposed to be in old cartoons meant for six-year-olds still puzzled us—and then Poteet went off in the direction of the Lodge to see if he could "scare anybody up," and I lay back again, resting my head on my rolled sleeping bag, and pulled a thick beach towel over me . . . I'm drowsy, and after a while find myself with DeannaDeannaDeanna in some nowhere where we are seated across from each other in a huge laundry tub filled two-thirds with warm water, Anna doesn't have a shirt on and her small perky breasts are dotted with perky nipples: "Keep pulling, Larry, keep pulling," she tells me, and dutifully I continue to tug on the cuffs of her wet jeans. The only landmark I recognize is the huge mulberry tree, which forms a kind of canopy over us.

Her jeans slip off entirely and I drop them outside the tub. Now she gets to her knees in the water—I see the dark V behind the wet fabric of her panties—and moves toward me, a hand outstretched, and I discover I'm naked and with a pulsing boner: and when her cold dripping hand touches me I explode, filling my head with a red haze, and I open my eyes at once and there I am on my cot, my hand around my cock, which is now deflating.

I lie there, faint, drowsing, in my wet-spotted skivvies until sometime later on (minutes? hours?) a sharp sound rouses me, a kind of growl. It comes again, and I suddenly recognize it, a siren, loud and near, but it's only just been barely tapped so it makes a couple of growling sounds without going into a wail: *Urrrrr . . . urrrrr* it goes again. Then nothing.

I look over to the other cot. Yeah, where the hell's Curly? Andy? Nick? Irving? Poteet? Crawley, Fangbone?

I get up, shuck out of my gummed-up skivvies, kick them under my cot, seek a clean pair from my duffel bag. And pull my shorts back on.

I leave the deserted pod and head toward the waterfront, the direction from which I thought those two warning growls of the siren, if that's what they were, had come.

The path is dark, but as I get closer, I see light ahead. I slow, trudge unwillingly forward, fearful there's something awful going on, yet I can't stop.

Then I come up on the rise just before the path descends all the way to the waterfront and see not one light but several; three powerful spotlights on tripods shoot yellow beams over the water as well as hitting the guardshack. There are red and white flashing lights on two blue and yellow state police cruisers; and in the midst of what resembles a lighted stage, figures pass to and fro, most with flashlights that seem to wink as they appear and disappear in the night.

And then I see the ambulance, stark white with black reversed lettering on its front, its red lights flashing soundlessly, its back door open as two state troopers bring forward a gurney on which a sheet-covered form rests; they fold the legs of the gurney up under it and lift the form up and slide it forward into the ambulance. When the door slams shut, all chatter and most movement cease.

A length of waterlogged rope now keeps the curious back from the guardshack and dock. Behind it are Poteet, Fangbone, and Crawley, and half a dozen others whose names I would ordinarily know but can't recall just now.

On the other side Bart, Bud, Nick, Perky, the knot-tying prof, the ROTC rifle-range guy, and a handful of other adults are on the scene—but most stand still dumbly, flat-footed, hands dangling uselessly at their sides, as if unable to decide if they are spectators or participants. One of the state police, the younger of the two, ducks under the rope, approaches Perky, they speak briefly, and the trooper moves away with that spruce almost cocky walk the always-trim state cops seem to have—local constables and sheriff's deputies tend to be big-bellied and look like they grunt when they walk.

"Christ, Jim, what's happening?" I ask Poteet.

"That was Andy that they put in the ambulance." Poteet's voice is higher than usual. His eyes are wild.

"God almighty . . . that can't *be*—" I don't know whether to cry, run, or stay where I am. "How bad is he hurt? And how did whatever happened happen?"

But before Poteet can answer me, Perky lifts the rope separating us, ducks under, and approaches us. I wonder why more guys haven't turned out—maybe the noise hadn't been sufficient to rouse them. Or maybe they heard *Urrrr . . . urrrrr,* but didn't give a rat's ass about anything beyond getting back to sleep.

Perky comes directly over to Poteet and me and puts a hand on each of our shoulders. His eyes are dark, wide, somber. He squeezes our shoulders. "Lads," he says, "Scouts," voice barely above a whisper. Then he turns to comfort and console other restless and frightened Scouts in the same fashion.

Seven

The air felt different as I slouched back to the pod alone, as if news of Andy's death had been sprayed like evil perfume upon the evening breezes and was even now descending upon everything along with the dew. A couple of times I heard wild shouts floating in from the direction of the waterfront, and once a high-pitched cry not far from a scream. But I kept walking, wanting to be away from the whole puzzling mess, to try to think. I'd been to funerals of older people from Ermine Falls and elsewhere in Skeegemog County—Gracious sang at many and I always liked to hear her—but I'd never known anyone my own age who'd died. I imagined Andy in his open coffin, his angelic face, the moans, weeping of his mother, father, beefy sisters, grandparents, and others from their numerous family.

Last fall Andy'd won second place in a talent show at Skeegemog high school playing "Bumble Boogie," which he'd taught himself, note by note, and the next day he played the piece in the upstairs eighth-grade homeroom during the last few minutes before lunch break was over.

Miller Springstead (awfully good on his Hohner harmonica) and I were the only guys interested enough to show up, but half a dozen senior girls were there, two cheerleaders, and four from the basketball team.

Andy sat at the piano talking to Ginnie Force, probably the best-looking girl in school, when his eyes found the clock on the wall. "Omigosh!"

He made a forty-five-degree turn on the stool and his left hand started the eight-to-the-bar bass, while his right became a delicate blur over the bumblebee part on the treble end, the two elements seeming to detonate somewhere above the old upright piano, where motes rose from the piano top . . . now both hands are at opposite ends of the keyboard and they begin to move to the middle by octaves, building to a crescendo, *Boom!* More dust rising from the piano. Then the bass beginning again under Andy's left hand, the right loosing the lively bumblebee again.

Breezes nudged trees, making a kind of sighing sound. The sound of my steps on the dirt path annoyed me. Insects weren't making much noise tonight, but I knew that in less than a month their night gratings, squeaks, chitterings, and shrills would begin to take on a frantic quality as the first frost approached. A scrap of moon like an illuminated fingernail clipping hung in the northwestern sky but sent small light and seemed largely lost amid the stars.

Nobody was stirring when I came to our pod, and I had no idea who might still be out and about and who was sawing wood. I felt more alone than at any time since I'd returned to Camp G.

I lay back on my cot, again propping my head against my rolled sleeping bag. I shivered and threw a thick towel over my bare legs, then began to drowse and would have fallen asleep had I not heard something nearby, like someone in the dark brushing against a tent. Then there was a scraping sound just outside.

The tent's flap was open about a quarter and I saw a beam of light shooting around outside. In a few moments the flap was pushed back and Curly was framed in the entrance, momentarily pointing his flashlight upward into his face for dramatic effect: the yellow light gave him a wolfish look and his shock of springy curls trembled. He was breathing audibly but didn't seem especially out of breath.

He came in, sat on his cot, let out a sigh of great relief, switched the flashlight off, and at once began talking rapidly, like an athlete exhilarated after a successful game: "Man, it was really something, huh? I mean, I heard and saw it *all,* Larry, I mean I heard this kid screaming his head off down by the dock and people trying to calm him down . . . he'd found Andy right there in the shallows by the shore, face down, Christ's teeth, the water was *only* about four or five inches deep there, but he musta got in trouble by swimming out into deep water, who knows, maybe he panicked and flailed around and ended up drowning and then his body musta washed into shore after a while? Right? Right!" He smacked a fist into his opposite palm and began to flash his light around in the tent. His excitement caused bright spots to surface in his cheeks, and in the flittering beam of his flashlight I watched for signs of sorrow or fear in his face but saw neither. I'd never seen him more animated.

I thought of Andy, still, silent, cold, by now probably whisked off to a morgue or funeral home. I felt something like outrage because it wasn't Curly who'd drowned—he was supposed to die early, so why wasn't it *him* who croaked in the water, not Andy, a pleasant kind so mild he'd shoo a mosquito from his arm rather than crush it, no nevermind that I didn't especially cotton to him.

"I saw you come down there a little later and stand around with Poteet and those other goofs, Larry, I was watching from behind that big tree to the west of the guardshack. You didn't get to see Andy when he was taken out of the water. Lemme tellya, it was awful to see them pull him out and roll him over on his back on the sand, his limbs all floppy as a Raggedy Andy's. Christ! He was such a touching little fucker too," Curly said. His voice slowed and deepened: "Maybe, you know, like ultimately, it was really too damn bad we both helped him make Swimmer, huh, Larry, 'cause otherwise he'd probably never have gone beyond his limit like that and he'd still be splashing around in the Beginner area like some lost baby seal . . . Larry? You got that look . . ."

"What look?"

"About believing me, about me being there to see and hear him get found . . . listen, Larry, if I tell you something else about it in confidence, will you keep a promise to never reveal it? Cross your heart'n hope to die?"

"Sure," I said without thinking.

"Okay, well, then, sorry to say, but I think I could be sorta responsible for him drowning—but only in a way, you understand, just sort of in a way, you see . . ."

"Sort of? In a way? What the hell's that mean?"

"Yeah, well, I know it prob'ly sounds a little funny . . . but maybe an hour before they found'im, Andy and I were down at the waterfront together—he wanted me to meet him there, invited me to sneak a nighttime swim, and he had something to talk over with me. So anyhow, we were standing in water about twenty feet from shore so it only came up to our thighs.

"Well, once Andy got going he was just a regular chatterbox, told me how good it was to have a pal like me, his 'comrade-in-arms' he called me, pretty creative, eh? And how he knew our friendship'd endure a lifetime, not end when our week together did. Christ, you'd a thought he was my fucking fiancée!

"So, I told'im: Like, hey, Andy, y'know, this is just a week at a dumb Scout camp, but yeah, sez I, I like you too, palzy, and we're all fine fellows and gentlemen scholars and all like that, and you, now you're one of my pals, of course you are, and I put an arm around his shoulders and said, 'You're okay, Andy! You're aces with me, buddy, now nuffa this, I gotta hustle back to the pod pretty soon.'

"And he said, 'Okay, I'm glad you feel that way,' and he put his lips to my cheek and then brought them around and pressed them right onto my lips! Like you'd kiss a girl! All that was missing was his tongue! And so I shoved'im over backward out into the drink . . . and when he stood up looking like a big baby, eyes like pie plates, I shit you none . . . thought he was gonna cry, you know . . . he came in closer. Sez he, 'But I . . . you . . . I . . . but I . . . I thought you *liked* me, *really* liked me . . .' and he started to move in slow motion toward the shore, but I didn't let'im get past me, see, I got in front of 'im and I shoved'im back out into the water . . . 'Stay the fuck out there,' I told'im, pushing him out into deeper water, 'You lied to me—you said you weren't a fucking fruit! A goddamn freaka nature!' 'Well,' he blubbers, 'But you *said* you really liked me! A lot! You *said*! A *lot*!' "

"Christ, how could you do that to him?" I said, awed by Curly's meanness.

"*How?* How could I *not?* Like I told you, he fucking *kissed* me, Larry! And right on the fucking lips too! What a fuck'm I 'sposed to do? I'm no goddamn fairy—what'd'ja expect me to do? French kiss'im? I told you long ago I suspected him of being queer. So when he started to come back to shore again, I got in his way, I pushed him back out into deep water, and when he came in next time I wouldn't let him past me, and after four or five tries he didn't try, just kinda floated around out there in water just a little over his head, maybe fifty feet out, treading water, looking at me like Kilroy . . . then I said, 'Okay, that's *enough*, c'mon in, Chrissake, I oughtn'ta done that, Andy,' and I backstroked a few yards toward shore . . . but now he got pissy and *wouldn't* come back, the stubborn prick, I dunno, probably he felt humiliated 'cause of trying that kinda homo crap on me, anyhow, whatever it was, he didn't say anything, he just stayed there, kind of floating, drifting, keeping quiet. I could hear him breathing. I dunno, anyhow I got so disgusted I just turned around and swam back in to shore and got my towel and never looked back and came back here and changed back into my clothes and then after a while I went back to the waterfront to see if the poor fucker was still out there, and it was then that I heard that kid hollering . . .''

"But didn't you go over and help?"

"Nah—wasn't any use, hell, I could tell from where I was that the way Andy was lying there on his back on the shore like a bag of sand showed that he was a goner . . . as dead as dead could be."

"But you can't . . . I mean, you coulda *tried!* Coulda tried that new kinda artificial respiration thing I was showing you! Maybe you coulda brought him back!"

"Oh, coulda done this, shoulda done that, Larry, Christ's teeth, Larry, you get some guy kinda slobbering and trying to smooch you and pawing after your dick, well, how much's a guy supposed to take? I mean, there's a limit . . ."

"I don't know," I said sullenly. "I've never really figured that one out either. But Jesus, Curly, you gotta tell Perky or the cops or somebody about meeting Andy there, and what happened and how he was when you left . . . and about coming back just when they were discovering him . . ."

"Oh, Christ, Larry, how fucking tiresome, I mean really . . ."

"Yeah, well, something about this thing isn't right," I said, realizing it's the first time I've ever said that to anybody. "Curly, we can't just shut up and walk away and leave poor fucking Andy looking like some asshole goof who fucked up—I dunno if anything you did or said mattered any, but I betcha somebody smarter'n the two of us together can likely figure it out and get things straight enough to tell Andy's ma and rest of his family what's what . . ."

 Curly looked almost bored: "I see no reason to say anything. But whatta *you* gonna tell'im, Larry? That it was nasty ole Curly did poor, pretty little Andy in? Kinda neat, there, Larry, I gotta admit, Why, you'd be a hero."

"No, I'd just tell'em what little I knew and let'em take it from there . . ."

"Well, however you cut it, old pal, you'd be the good guy blowin' the whistle on evil old Curly . . . well, Larry, old sport, I guess I'd just have to tell'em I *was* there, and so were you, and it was *you*, not *me*, who pushed li'l ole Chubby out to sea, that it was *you* told *me* what you'd done and threatened to blame *me* for it if *I* didn't keep *my* mouth shut—and, hey, you already know what a fan*tastic* liar I am, Larry, Christ, I've never known *any*one half as good as me at it . . . maybe it's because I like to mix lies in with the truth in such a way that I talk myself into believing my own yarn myself—sincerity is what I got, and whatever I come up with, Larry, you know I'll deliver it with my winningest smile my most earnest look and sincerest voice . . . hey, look down at your feet, Larry . . ."

I do.

Curly puts index and middle fingers together, sticks them under my nose, and jerks them up, bringing a sharp stab of pain to my nose as my head flies up and my eyes water so I can barely see. I step back from him, have to wipe my eyes on the back of my hand,

and when I next look up, Curly's towering over me, sneering down on me: and with no more warning than a strangled cry, I hurl myself upon him, knocking him back onto his cot, I leap on top of him, hold him down with my knees on his shoulders as he tried to wriggle away, then my hands of their own accord encircle his long thin muscular neck and tighten and tighten, thumbs digging into his throat, his arms flailing wildly, then he seizes my wrists, but I'm way too strong and enraged for him and I squeeze and squeeze and listen to him gasp and gag as he tries to suck in some wind, then his hands go slack and drop from my wrists: and I come back to myself a bit and release him, and horrified and shaking, climb off him and stand, trembling, looking down as he gasps and at last draws in deep breaths and massages his throat which now has angry red splotches where my hands had been . . . I say nothing, am sort of gasping myself.

It takes Curly maybe a couple minutes to get his breathing and gasping to throttle down.

When he's able to sit up, he swings his legs around and plants them on the floor. I'm waiting to deal with rage and hate but instead Curly smiles . . . and unsteadily sticks his hand out and deliberately pats the front of my shorts. "Why, Larry," he rasps, "I didn't know you cared." He's smiling as he lazily points to where my shorts bulge from half a boner.

He turns away from me then, and begins patting and touching the marks my fingers made on his neck. "Y'know," he says, his voice hoarse and grainy but cheerful, "when you have your little chat with Perky or the sheriff or state cops or whoever, then I guess I'll have no choice but to show them what you've done to me, you know, to keep me from spilling the beans. God, Larry, I just can't imagine *how* things are gonna work out for you . . . whadda *you* think? Huh?"

I don't answer. So here's the Curly I'd always suspected had lain beneath the chatter and curls and strange hates and games and taunts and lies. And what *would* happen if he presented himself to Perky, protesting his assault by me, pointing to his blotched throat—the ease with which he'd tricked me begins to reignite my rage, but this time I keep the lid on.

Curly lets it all sink in a little more, then says, "Well, what the hell, Larry, tell you what, my old pal, for old time's sake I won't say anything if you don't. My policy is, Ask me no questions and I'll tell you no lies. Live and let live! Laissez-goddamn-faire, right? Hey, whaddya say we go get us some breakfast, man, I could eat a horse, all this fuckin' around's makin' me hungry, no shit. Just let me grab my turtleneck shirt, I know it's here somewhere. Oh, yeah, and Larry—y'know about my nigger jokes?"

"Yeah?"

"Well, just so you know, that was all just bullshit too—hell, old buddy, I don't hate boogies, I *love* boogies! Honest Injun! Hey, you hear the one about the queer bear? Tried to lay his paw on the table . . . or about the queer snake that tried to rape a rope . . ." He finishes pulling on a sky-blue cotton turtleneck shirt he'd gotten from his duffel bag. It nicely hides the marks I'd put on his neck. "I knew this fucker'd come in handy."

Just before he ducks out through the flap, he stops dead, turns, eyes fixed on me: "And another thing, Larry, I don't really hate queers either. I can tell you suspect I might be one, and that's okay— but for your information, I *ain't-ain't-ain't!* Oh, and another thing, Larry: I go for the girls, just like you do, pal—*just* like you do . . ."

Eight

Breakfast was a pretty gloomy affair. I'd expected excited chatter about last night, maybe tears and eyes avoiding mine, but silence and glumness marked the meal. Most kept their heads down as they dug into little waxed boxes of cereal which they sugared heavily and added milk to. Very few went through the serving line to get hotcakes, eggs, sausage, and bacon—but Poteet, Curly, and I approached it eagerly, and we loaded our plates with fried eggs, bacon, sausage, and hotcakes and at the table ate so hungrily we didn't speak and didn't pay attention to much except the food. I hadn't been so hungry in a long time. I had to force myself to stop eating.

Just as Fangbone and Crawley were getting up to leave, Perky appeared in the main entrance to the dining hall, looking like he'd aged five years overnight.

He strode quickly to the head of the room and stood before us in yesterday's wrinkled shorts and shirt. The vertical lines on his face looked like they'd been etched with a chisel, His eyes were pouched and bloodshot.

"Lads," he began slowly, "truly, there's nothing sadder on earth than the death of a young man in the very acme of his life, both for him and his family. I have myself suffered the death of a child in years past, and I can report that it's something you never fully recover from. Being the parent left behind can be a horror. If there's any consolation to be found in all this, perhaps it's best captured in a single line from the Welsh poet Dylan Thomas's 'A Refusal to Mourn the Death, by Fire, of a Child in London.'" He paused, then recited the short line in a slow deep somber voice: "'After the first death, there is no other.'"

He waited a few moments, then continued, "Further, I hope these lines from Matsunaga Teitoku may provide some small comfort for we who grieve:

"*The morning glory blooms but an hour*
And yet it differs not at heart
From the giant pine that lives for a thousand years . . .

"I'm grateful to be able to inform you the authorities suspect no foul play in this tragic and hideous accident; in truth, that would have been a moral insult too severe for us to brook, I fear, and would validate these words from the sixth-century Roman philosopher Boethius, whom I've lately been rereading: 'The desire to do evil may be due to human weakness; but for the wicked to overcome the innocent in the sight of God—that is monstrous.' And now let Boethius, a man imprisoned and tortured to death by the Romans, provide our concluding prayer: 'Ruler of all things, calm the roiling waves and, as you rule the immense heavens, rule also the earth in stable concord.' Having entered into eternal life, our comrade Andy is henceforth exempt from further pain, but let us bear ours with humility and remembrance. Now, we bid our fallen companion farewell. I know you're all accustomed to hearing Taps as either a recording or occasionally live from a bugler, but today, though it's morning, I propose to sing the first stanza of the lyrics for Taps for you—you can think of it as 'Taps at Reveille,' an F. Scott Fitzgerald title, as it happens:

"*Day is done*
gone the sun
from the lakes

from the hills
from the sky
all is well
safely rest
God is nigh . . .

"Now, lads, we'll all assemble by the flagpole at 9:30, just thirty minutes from now, in full uniform, and you'll be bussed in to town for the parade. I understand we won't be far behind the wonderful Boy Scout Drum and Bugle Corps from Racine, Wisconsin. They're a fine group, and very worthy of their reputation, as you'll see and hear."

As we walked back toward our pod, Curly began to sing, to the tune of "Margie":

"Orgy, I want a real george orgy,
You bring benzedrine and rye
And I'll bring Spanish fly . . .
I'll have a real george orgy with yewww . . ."

He mock-punched me on the shoulder: "I knew this damn turtleneck'd come in handy . . . you still sore at me, Larry?"

"Nah . . . I shouldn't've hauled off and jumped you like that, I guess . . . I'm sorry . . . sometimes some kinda pissed-offedness just sweeps over me like there's some kinda red wire lashing around inside my head . . ."

"Nuff said. Apology accepted. Pals again?"

"Sure, pals again," I said, thinking of the plaster plaque in my bedroom at home: the lanky hound, the half-naked curly-top, his arm around the dog's left front leg.

Of course we have to shake on it. I don't have the strength to not take his hand. Curly's grip is firm as ever. He must sense I fear the aftermath of accusing him more than I need justice for Andy.

"Hey, Larry, I'm gonna skip down to the commissary and get us each a coupla Milky Ways . . . how's that sound? A little sugar can be a real good thing on a morning like this."

"Sounds good. Thanks."

"Don't mention it. Gotta hustle to get over there and back and get suited up. Wonder why the bastards hardly ever have Tootsie Rolls? I'll betcha there's some bastard gets in early when the Tootsie Rolls come in and then hogs 'em all . . ."

When I got to the pod, I found Gracious and Jeanine Dellums, Andy's mother, standing by our tent, looking around.

Vera and June Dellums, Jeanine's bulky daughters, seventeen and eighteen, gripped their mother on either side by her arms, though their support was very light and it was more a comforting grip than something to keep her upright. Still, Jeanine, a few years younger than Gracious, olive-skinned and dark-haired, plump like the rest of the family, looked as though she'd slip to the ground were the hands withdrawn.

"Oh, Larry!" Gracious closed the space between us rapidly and took me in her arms. She'd been crying, was weepy still. Then she held me at arm's length and we both turned our heads to look at the three Dellumses: they were all hefty, wore sack-like flower-printed dresses and looked more like sisters than sisters and mother.

I knew I should say something but couldn't seem to get anything out. But when Gracious looked at me sharply, I called over, "I'm so sorry, Missus Dellums . . . you too, Vera and June . . . we're all just awful sad . . . we liked Andy and awful, awful lot . . ."

"Thank you," Jeanine said, just loud enough for us to hear.

"Larry," Gracious said quietly, "Jeanine's here to get Andy's belongings . . . do you know where the are?"

I pointed at Andy's and Poteet's tent.

"Is his roommate in?"

"I don't think so." I hadn't seen Poteet since breakfast, had no idea where he might be.

"Well, would you go look—if he's there, maybe you and he can gather up Andy's things—if he's not, why don't you just go ahead and do it?"

"Okay . . ."

Inside, the tent felt cold, as if it hadn't had an occupant in a week. Poteet's stuff was all neatly arranged on and under his cot.

Just about all of Andy's stuff was on his cot in meager disorderly piles except for his Scout uniform, which was folded neatly, ready for use in the Cherry Festival parade. His cap, belt, clean Fruit of the Looms, and socks lay atop trousers and shirt. The contents of his pockets were in a little round pile: Scout knife; three dimes, a quarter, and two pennies; a leather billfold, very thin; an unopened pack of Wrigley's Spearmint; half a roll of cherry Life Savers. I could feel my jaws begin to ache. When I emerged from the tent with all the things put into Andy's duffel bag (its bottom half had already been filled with dirty clothes), Gracious had taken June's place beside her mother. Vera stood ready at the tent flap to receive whatever I'd gathered. "Say, Vera, can I carry this to wherever your car is?" I asked. "It'll be no trouble at all . . ."

"Thank you, Larry. No, I'd . . . I'd like to take the things myself, but thank you, Larry, thank you very much." She held the duffel bag against her, hugging it as if it were alive, her countenance so sorrowful it was painful to see, and when she lifted her head and looked me in the eyes, her sorrow made me look away.

Curly got back with the candy bars just as Gracious and the Dellumses were disappearing in the direction of the waterfront. "Told ya so—no goddamn Tootsie Rolls again. That early-bird son-ofabitch musta got 'em. Pisses me off. Here—" He tossed me two Milky Ways.

"Thanks."

Since Curly didn't seem inclined to ask about the Dellumses, I didn't tell him anything and was grateful he hadn't got back sooner. I didn't want Andy's family and Curly to meet.

"Thanks a lot," I said, taking the candy bars. "I owe you two."

"Forget it," he said. "Hey, guess we better get a hustle on, we only got fifteen minutes to get dressed and get down to catch the bus."

"Right."

"Still pals, right? You knew I was just fooling with you about going against you, right?"

"Sure thing," I said, tearing the wrapper from my first Milky Way. "Pals still." I was tremendously eager to sink my teeth into the candy bar.

"Guess that was Andy's mom and sisters with your mom, huh? I could see the family resemblance. The mother looked like she was feeling pretty bad."

"Yeah, we all were. Are."

"Well," Curly said, "now is a good time to have a pal, that's for sure."

"Yeah."

I bit savagely into the Milky Way and the sweetness of the chocolate and caramel almost overwhelmed me, but at the same time it was good, good.

Nine

I shift from foot to foot. Heat from the pavement penetrates my soles. From all over needles of bright light burn into me, glancing blows of sun bounced from windows, cars, parking meters, anything that's vaguely shiny, here on Railroad Avenue, from which our part of the parade will enter the main drag, East Front Street. We twenty-odd Scouts are assembled four abreast, ready to march.

Floats from our side are to merge with others assembled on Sunset Park, just across East Front Street from us.

There's a good breeze coming off Grand Traverse Bay and flowing across my burning skin. And I have my Scout cap on—otherwise it'd feel like the damned sun was boring a hole in my skull. My neckerchief helps shade my neck. I can feel the tops of my ears start to burn. Sweat trickles down my sides and into my skivvies.

Curly, to my right, turns toward me. He seems to tower over me: "Hey, Larry, y'hear 'bout the kid in school telling his teacher how his parents ate light bulbs?"

"Can't say's I have . . ." Those angry marks I left on his neck have pretty much subsided by now, though a purplish one the size of a thumb is still visible just above his collarbone.

" 'Why,' the teacher says, 'Johnny, that's absurd!' 'No, it ain't,' he claims. 'Ever' night I hear Paw say, "Turn out the light, Maw, and let's eat it." ' "

Laughter stirs in my belly, it wants to worm its way up into my throat, then burst coarsely forth like vomit, but I manage to fight it down.

The rest of the guys look restless, hot, and bored, but kind of eager too for the thing to begin, the better to get it over with. Fangbone is AWOL, but Steve Crawley is here, looking sad and bedraggled.

We'd gotten here quickly in the Camp G school bus and gone immediately to our designated spot, the next-to-last spot at parade's end.

Immediately behind us, almost the last of the parade, is a gag band of goofs of some kind, half a dozen big-gutted middle-aged guys done up in women's clothes—slips, bathing suits, floor-length dresses, wigs, pedal pushers. Some wear stuffed gigantic bras. They're tuning their instruments, playing a few bars of "You Are My Sunshine," their already-bright faces daubed with lipstick. Vivid spots of rouge on their cheeks are almost fluorescent in the dreadful sun. One guy is tootling some kind of pleasant air on a recorder, but the other scrapings pretty much drown it out.

Another guy, wearing bloomers, a blonde wig, and a huge red brassiere, obviously the one you'd call Life of the Party, blows a fart noise on his trumpet, and for some reason I think of the guys' legs athwart the stern gunwales, pumping their canoes like they're trying to hump the water, on Waterfront Night when I screwed up my race, and how Curly just behind me'd whispered, " 'Course you realize the guy wins who can blow the most farts to move him along . . ."

There are many floats and noisy marching bands ahead of us— being next to the very end of the parade lets us see what's going on fairly far ahead of us as floats and bands make the turn onto East Front: songs like "You Are My Sunshine," which the goofs behind us have blasted into, vie with Sousa marches and military anthems farther down the line.

Not all that far ahead of us we can see G. Mennen "Soapy" Williams, our governor, driven by a state trooper in a long cream-colored Cadillac convertible, seated next to a dark-haired, dark-complected slender woman, doubtless his wife. I'm surprised he's not nearer the front of the parade.

Finally our contingent starts to move toward spectators lined up on either side of East Front just ahead of us, and Soapy and his woman are already practicing a few waves and smiles. Soapy is sure a handsome guy, if also a little daffy-looking. His long black silver-streaked hair is swept straight back, and he grins wildly at everything in all directions. He has a great toothy smile.

Blair Moody, a balding, middle-aged Michigan senator, comes behind Soapy, likewise in a convertible, this time a red Chevy, driven by a young woman in a mauve dress. We get a good view as he makes the left turn onto East Front.

Several floats now moving slowly forward feature girls in bathing suits cradling baskets of flowers to toss to the audience when things get further underway.

Far ahead I glimpse a float with a huge and somewhat stumpy effigy of Père Marquette. But as far as I'm concerned, the only thing much worth looking at after Soapy is the all-white National Cherry Queen float, perhaps twenty yards ahead of us, bearing the queen, Clover La Baugh, from Traverse City, and also the daughter of the family that owns Les Champs du Roi, the resort on Lake Albion near our home in Ermine Falls where Gracious works summers, keeping the books and even sometimes substituting for the hostess in the dining room.

Clover is just about the most beautiful young woman I've ever seen, and she's especially animated today: all in white, her puffy skirt billows in the breeze, her short blonde hair frames her oval glowing face, and even at this distance I can tell her pretty red mouth is wide with pleasure and excitement.

Following Clover comes a "cowgirl," wearing a skimpy fringed skirt and halter and ten-gallon hat, walking beside her bay horse, looking about ready to mount.

Nick and Irwin have been standing a bit apart from us, talking to Perky. The red scratch Irwin got on Wednesday's hike is still there, and is maybe a little worse-looking. Perky looks toward the group of us, says something to Nick, as he and Irwin approach us.

"Lookit that prick," Poteet mutters, referring to Irwin. "Looks like he's got a poker up his ass."

Nick and Irwin begin to get us into shape. Now that we are reduced to twenty-five from defections of Scouts not bothering with the parade and leaving early, we slide almost naturally into five rows of five Scouts each. Behind us a member of the band of goofs rips off a belch as loud as a shout.

Not a sign, of course, of Bart or Bud—when I'd gone to the waterfront to say goodbye, they were in a near-frenzy of getting their stuff together so they could get the hell out of Camp G as fast as possible, their eyes bright with eagerness to be gone as they grabbed up clothing and other items, cramming all recklessly into duffel bags. But Bart hadn't been in such a hurry that he didn't take time to warn me: "Keep your eye on the goofball Curly, Larry. Anybody with half a brain can see that prick's bad news, always stirring things up, getting some kind of bullshit going so he can sit back and watch what he's set in motion like some kind of goddamn movie director . . ." He'd given me a quick hug instead of a handshake and muttered, "Take care, pal, take care . . . don't take any wooden nickels . . ."

"You too," I got out, voice thick with sorrow at seeing him go.

And now Bart's gone back to the University of Florida, and I somehow know I will never see him again.

Just ahead of us, starting to blast out a Sousa march, goes the outfit we follow, probably making us look like we're there to pick up anything they might drop, because our forerunner is the famous Racine Drum & Bugle Corps revered by Perky and many others—CHAMPIONS OF SCOUTING runs the legend on their biggest drum, beaten by a brutish-looking Scout who somewhat resembles Poteet. So we have a champion drum and bugle corps before us while behind us come the goof-offs, the fuck-ups, the renegades, the men-dressed-as-women band (not quite a band, actually: bass drum, snare drum, trumpet, accordion, and trombone). I see Life of the Party has a big shiny harmonica on a chain around his neck—maybe that counts for an instrument too.

We can see floats and bands and other attractions moving forward before us on East Front Street, and before long the Racine Drum & Bugle Corps steps smartly off, and we follow, not even needing Nick's strident *"Scouts, for'd harch!"* We straighten up, we throw our shoulders back, we march. For now I quit gawking at the parade's attractions and pretty much pay attention to getting and keeping in step as we approach the spectator-lined street. For a while Nick does his idiotic "Hup-hoop-hu-reep-foah!" as we press on, adding our own splotch of khaki drabness to the great noisy colorful moving clot of the parade. The noise is tremendous and is everywhere. Irwin slyly fingers his wounded cheek.

The Racine group is just drumming for now, and behind us we can hear the trick band picking up a bit and the fat trumpeter Life of the Party sings in a loud hard flat voice:

> *"Oh, we went to the animal fair,*
> *The birds and the beasts were there,*
> *The big baboon, by the light of the moon*
> *Was combing his auburn hair . . ."*

About halfway into the parade I see Gracious in the crowd lining East Front with her 8mm Kodak movie camera, shooting us, and me in particular, her platinum hair shining in the morning sun, all hopeful and trying to smile, but clearly sad about Andy at the same time.

The lens is pointed right at me so I offer up a goofy smile and wave, which causes me to get a bit out of step. I have to admit it warms me to see her there, taking my picture. Then I am swept along again, a scale bound to the snake.

Nick is marching before us, carrying Boy Scout and Camp Greavey and U.S. flags while Irving walks alongside, eyes peeled for anyone out of step.

For most of us, the parade's novelty pretty much wears off at about what must be the two-thirds point: my feet are burning in my heavy official Boy Scout shoes, I have dinner plates of sweat under my arms just like my fellow Scouts, and sweat trickles annoyingly down my back. My companions are likewise bedraggled—not a murmur from Curly, whose eyes appear glazed with boredom and fatigue— and I can see whatever hole our group is filling in the scheme of things is pretty damn small, pretty minor, and the parade wouldn't have lost a single damn thing by our absence. Christ, who could care about a ragtag bunch of kids in silly uniforms, most about half-way into their teens, when there are cars and horses and bare-armed and -legged girls strutting their stuff, especially the baton twirlers leading some of the bands? On the parade wound like some gigantic centipede of which we might make up a foot and a half a leg.

When we are on the last 200 yards from our destination of Railroad Street, the troupe of goofs behind us blasts into an energetic version of "When the Saints Go Marching In." In the middle, there's a sudden short interlude where all instruments, even snare and bass drums, go silent, and the music is supplied by Life of the Party alone, playing hauntingly on his big gleaming harmonica.

It's the best thing I've heard all day.

They play nothing for a time as we all march along purposefully, and when we are in sight of Railroad Street and can see, in the distance, the Camp G bus, the drummer does a little wind-up and Life of the Party, burly and gravel-voiced, completes lyrics he'd begun earlier:

> "*The monkey he got drunk!*
> *And sat on the elephant's trunk!*
> *The elephant sneezed and fell to his knees*
> *And that was the end of the monk!*
> *The monk! The monk! The monk!*
> And that was the end of the monk!"

Life of the Party, catching me watching him, shakes his head so his yellow curls bounce, then gives me a wink and a thumbs-up.

By the time we reach our bus we're all sweaty and tired and cranky even though we've really only marched for a little over two hours. Every time I blink my head is full of afterimages.

On the trip back in the bus we're all curiously subdued, sullen and silent, as though we'd run a long slow footrace and now want nothing more than to forget all about it.

Curly and I sit on the same seat near the back. He has the window seat and is the only one of us who shows much interest in what's outside. Behind us I heard one kid tell another, "A gorp is somebody who sits in a bathtub, lets farts, and bites the bubbles."

I'm not interested enough to turn and look for the author. Ordinarily I'd expect Curly to turn around and start jabbering, but he keeps his gaze fixed on the outside.

About halfway back to the pod I come upon a stocky man, his back to me, standing in the middle of the trail, looking toward our pod. Somehow he senses I'm behind him because he quickly turns to directly face me, looks me up and down, and says, "Say, there, son, excuse me, but might you be Larry Carstairs?"

I'm surprised but not astonished. "I am."

He puts out his hand and I take it. He's not a tall man but he's very wide and his fingers are thick as sausages. His whole bearing suggests solidity. Of course I recognized Vartan Norrys as soon as I saw him.

He stands before me, lightly sweating, wearing a tufted gray suit that gleams a bit in the sun like Gracious's hair and looks like silk. There are no cuffs on his pants and he wears rather pointed black shoes so bright you can see your face in them. His shirt is deep purple, his tie a shaft of burnt orange. He has a fine head of thick wavy dark hair combed straight back.

"Well, I'm your roommate's dad, Larry—Bob Norrys. Rusty wrote me about you. I'm glad he found a friend here—he may be a bright, attractive kid, but he doesn't have that many real friends or at any rate any close ones—Rusty actually described you in a letter well enough so I'd know you when I saw you . . ."

Though he probably could play a movie gangster as Poteet had suggested, "Bob" Norrys has what I guess you'd call a cultured voice; I can imagine Gracious saying of him, "He enunciates so beautifully!"

"He must be a pretty good writer." A sharp piney scent of cologne or aftershave drifts into my nostrils.

"Well, the lad definitely has some talent with prose—I just hope he stays with it, though I think he's possibly more drawn to acting. He likes to do impersonations. Zany improvisations. He tells me he has everybody here calling him 'Curly,' what a cut-up, eh? But he can be fickle and more than a little capricious sometimes if he doesn't get immediate results like he wants. At any rate, he described you as 'the most wonderfully alert guy I've met in a long time,' which is high flattery from him."

"Gosh, I guess so."

"Say, do you happen to know where my prodigal son might be at the moment, Larry?"

"Well, I think he headed up to the Lodge to see if he can find this guy Jerry who works in the kitchen to tell him goodbye."

"So he should be back at his tent shortly?"

"Yessir. Probably in minutes."

"Oh, Christ, don't call me sir, Larry, I don't much like formality—Bob's fine."

"Yeah, sure thing, anyhow he should be here in a few minutes—want me to run up to the Lodge and find him, um, Bob?"

"Nah, don't bother—this'll give us an opportunity to chat for a few minutes. As I say, I'm glad you've befriended my boy . . . he doesn't, ah, gravitate toward too many people, and I always consider it a victory when he finds someone he likes and establishes a rapport with . . . so how's he been doing?"

"Aneurysm? Marfan's syndrome?" Bob Norrys laughed heartily and I half-expected him to slap his knee. "No, you see, what's happened here, I'm afraid, is that my lovely little wretch has gone and appropriated parts of good Lovell Gibb's medical history. What a story thief he is, the little fraud! Guess it kind of goes with his creativity. And of course he's an only child. Lovell's my late wife's brother, you see, and he *does* suffer from Marfan's and so is indeed at risk for aneurysms. And say, I'm glad to've learned Lovell's finally revealed the secret of his first name—what a sterling gent he is! Old school!

They don't make 'em like that these days! Well, hell, Rusty may even work up a version of *you,* Larry, before he's done, you know, for his future work. What a card that kid can be! A 'caution,' as they used to say. Well, I do want to reassure you, Larry . . . Rusty's basically harmless, you just need to know how extremely much he enjoys embroidering and playing with the truth—you see, it's really an acting challenge sort of thing, I think, you know, playing a role to see what kind of a response he can get from his audience—can't seem to help it, you see. Of course I'm a little uncertain about his, ah, how shall I say it, uh, call it his identity in the, uh, pantheon of the sexes—but let's be positive, he's quicksilver, that boy, one in a million. One of these days he'll surely figure it all out by himself . . . you agree?"

"You bet," I say, hoping there's something like conviction in my voice. "He's going somewhere, that's for sure." I'm still surprised at Bob's frankness and ease when he speaks to me, basically a kid, after all.

"Well, thanks for your reinforcement, Larry . . . but tell you what, it occurs to me that maybe I've been a bit overly frank discussing Rusty and Lovell just now, so about our little conversation here, well, if you don't mind, I won't mention it if you won't . . . but, really, just remember you'll want to take some of his yarns with the proverbial grain of salt. Not all, but some, and that can make things a little confusing."

"Suits me." And it does—I'd already decided the same thing and hoped to just try to henceforth take Curly mostly for his entertainment value . . . and take care to not get tangled up further with the bastard. I wish I could rid myself of the thought that Curly may have killed Andy, but I can't, even though I've concluded all that stuff about pushing Andy back out into the water was probably bullshit.

I can't help asking Bob a final question: "Did he go to boarding school in Switzerland?"

"Ha ha ha! No, he goes to St. George's prep school in Portsmouth, Rhode Island . . . though I did once take him to Switzerland with me on a job . . . think we were there about a week and a half—what'd he say?"

"Just that he went to school there and could speak French."

"Typical of the kid: he'll tell you all this stuff, then omit the one thing that has some relevance to the truth. What a sense of irony! But he *can* speak French, though he's not quite what you'd call entirely fluent. Ha. In ways more than one, eh, Larry?"

But I don't get to answer with more than a nod, for here comes Curly now, no, "Rusty," accompanying Gracious, who's laughing at something he's just said. Curly's face is bright with joy in entertaining her. And Gracious is stimulated as well.

"Hi," Curly greets us, "glad to see you two are getting acquainted."

Gracious smiles at Bob Norrys, then at me.

Gracious and Bob chat easily as I'd thought would be the case, neither of them hogging the stage, each with a question or two for the other—I see this in a single backward glance as Curly and I move off until we've turned a bend in the path and are out of their line of sight. Then we stop.

"Well, what'd you think of the old man?" Curly asks casually, but I can see he's very alert as he waits for my answer.

"Oh, a real nice guy—told me to call him Bob. And I guess he calls you Rusty . . ."

"Ah, his common-touch schtick-thing again. Sure, why not call him Bob, a good-as-gold American name as there is, and not a foreigny one like Vartan—t'ain't good fer bidness, don'tcher know? I guess I sometimes just like to fool around with different names when I go places where people don't know me. Hey, maybe I'll discover I really am a Curly and make it permanent. My first name really *is* Russell, though, like I told you our first day."

"And so I guess Perky's actually your uncle, eh?"

"Hey, I didn't say anything or call him Uncle Perkins or anything, people'd've thought I was tryinna get special treatment or something . . . that'd go against his grain . . ."

"Yeah?"

"Yeah. Mine too."

"Your dad said Perky's the guy with that syndrome thing."

"Well, he is . . . but it runs in the family, I got the trait too, from Mom, she carried it'n I may well have it . . . feels like it sometimes . . ."

"Feels like it?"

"Oh, sure, you can actually feel the bulge on your ascending aorta, Larry, if it's up around, say, four centimeters long, if you press your chest wall . . ."

"No shit." His answers for everything are actually, for the first time, beginning to bore me.

"Hey, let's walk up by the rifle range . . . few things I wanta talk over with you—'cause looks like this is it, eh, old buddy, as they say in the movies, here's where we part company, Larry, you go your way and I go mine—look, you want to keep in touch? Write letters? Who knows, maybe we're not done with each other quite yet . . ."

"Sure thing," I say, meaning it, because I'm curious to find out how he'd express himself on the page. "I get a kick out of getting letters and I always write back pretty quick."

We take the fork toward the rifle range.

"That's great, but hey, about this kinda compulsion I have to, uh, 'embroider' events, as Bob would probably say, you gotta understand, it's not for self-aggrandizement or because of some pathological compulsion to *lie*, no, my impulse is basically artistic: I wanta write stories, plays, maybe a novel, so I'm always cooking up little things I might use . . . I like bending and twisting things and making up new facts and seeing people's faces react when I spring something really outrageous on them . . . but like I already told you, I guess I don't *really* hate anything or anybody, really—queers and boogies and all that are actually perfectly fine with me, guess I just look at 'em as material to fool around with when I'm talking or writing, you know?"

"Yeah," I say, even though I don't. And I almost hate myself because still, even after considering Curly might be a murderer of some kind, I can't help sort of liking something about the crazy bastard, or at least a major part of him—even as I sort of fear him (why I don't know).

"Well, I guess this is it, Larry . . ."

I look back up the trail to see if Bob Norrys and Gracious might be ambling back this way, but there's no one.

"I packed my stuff and put it in Bob's car earlier, Larry, so I guess I'll say goodbye and head back."

Curly extends his long-fingered deceptively strong right hand, and we both squeeze hard. Then, tears in his eyes—I wonder if they're real or if he's so good he can summon them up at will—he breaks from me and runs off awkwardly back the way we'd come, where Bob Norrys (or Vartan Norrys, who knows) waits for him.

He stops once, turns, and calls back, his voice suddenly shaking with emotion, "We'll write, Larry, we'll write! We have to! And we won't forget! Remember, we're both only children! With only one parent! We're brother atheists, you and me! We're both creative personalities!"

"So long," I call, but he's already gone. I remember that he hasn't given me his address and I haven't given him mine.

I don't like admitting it, but my world seems just a little shrunken with Curly gone from it.

Still, it'd be like him to find out my address later on—it wouldn't be hard—and then write me—or show up—when he thinks he might most catch me unawares. And then he'd tell me all over again about the ambiguity of just about everything.

Ten

I stood in the living room before the sunroom's entrance. Gracious had left both French doors open for circulation and the house felt cool and comfortable, yet somehow almost alien. It was hard to explain. It was the same, yet everything seemed just a little different. I thought of the Ray Bradbury story of a time traveler who on his trip to prehistoric times had stepped briefly off a walkway over the land, a forbidden act he kept secret; and when he got back, everything was different: air, colors, and so on . . . and upon looking at his mud-clotted boot he discovered a beautiful prehistoric butterfly embedded there.

The other set of south-facing French doors that opened onto the cement porch were slightly open so I opened them further and drank in the breezes. I turned and stood, looking about. On the western wall, just below the French windows, was a bricks-and-boards bookcase. The top shelf contained my favorites: *Shallow Water Diving, Best American Humorous Short Stories, Secret Sea* by Robb White, *Double Trouble* by Charles Lee Bryson, a few Thornton Burgess and other books left over from childhood. My favorite was a paperback with *Call of the Wild* and *White Fang* in one volume. I badly wanted a dog but Gracious wouldn't hear of it ("Who'd take care of it if we took a trip someplace?"), and suggested a compromise of a guinea pig. ("They're nice and clean, and you can carry them wherever you go in a cage.")

I turned until I faced east: before me, my rolltop desk, a relic from the Sinclair station, which Gracious had sold not long after news of my father's death. Above it on the wall my prints of Bambi and Thumper whose outlines used to glow in the dark. I turned north: atop my pine chest of drawers sits my eyeless (unless you count the yarn Xs) teddy bear.

On my right, my army surplus bunk with the mattress Gracious wanted to replace for the very reason I insist on keeping it. Over the years my body had made a kind of valley in its middle, and it always feels good to roll into it at night.

On the north wall above where my head was when I read or slept was my favorite object, a plaster of Paris plaque: an almost-naked boy sits on what looks like a stone bench, his arm around the left front leg of a lanky, friendly-looking hound. The inscription at the plaque's base reads "PALS."

I step through the French doors, push open the screen door, and step out onto the porch. Though the dimming sun doesn't pack much heat right now, its earlier warmth is still embedded in the thick concrete and it feels good on my bare soles, unlike the blazing pavement of the Cherry Festival parade.

I look down and on the first step below the porch, I see something, and my heart lurches: lying there is a bouquet only Deanna could have left: daisies, black-eyed Susans and Indian paintbrush, arranged so that from the center the hardy burnt orange and scarlet of the paintbrush melts out into the Susans while the outer rim of daisies is like the sun's corolla. It reminds me of a color photo I once saw of a spiral galaxy. A nearly invisible thread keeps the stems together.

I bring Anna's creation in, put it in a slender pewter vase of Gracious's—she's in her bedroom with the door almost closed—and am about to set it on the dining room table when I change my mind and go back to the sunroom and put it on top of the dresser next to my teddy bear. When as an infant I gnawed its eyes off, I was bereft until Gracious made yarn Xs to replace them.

I see no reason to share Anna's bouquet with Gracious or answer any questions it might raise.

"So we'll have a little sort of luncheon for supper tonight, Larry. I really don't like much on my stomach when I'm going to sing, but we'll both still want to take some nourishment."

I'd often wondered why Gracious likes words like "buffet" and "luncheon" and phrases like "taking nourishment." I think of Perky and his "Taps at Reveille."

Gracious and several members of the Church of Christ choir she leads are going over to the Deer Rapids church a dozen miles away to practice tonight because, she told me, "the acoustics are so lovely."

She goes into the kitchen and starts preparing our food. I hear her begin to hum as she works, a sound I've always liked, and I move to the entrance between dining room and kitchen. She's humming "Shall We Gather at the River," then she sings a few bars: "Yes, we'll gather at the river . . . the beau-ti-ful river . . . Oh, I've always loved that one . . . do you remember 'In the Garden,' Lamar . . . I'm sorry, Larry . . ."

"Yeah . . ."

"Oh, sing along with me just a little."

"Okay."

And we do harmonize pretty well:

*"I come to the garden alone
While the dew is still on the ros-es
And the voice I hear,
Falling on my ear,
The Son of God dis-closes
And He walks with me
And He talks with me,
And he tells me I am His own"*

"Oh, that was so nice, Larry, you could develop a lovely voice if you ever wanted to . . ." Her pretty face turns sorrowful. "I'm just so glad we're all Christians, Lamar, and know we're assured of eternal life, but even so I still can't get poor Andy's face out of my mind . . . Jeanine and the girls are still just absolutely *stricken* . . ."

Our "sort of luncheon" turns out to be hamburgers, a pineapple-ring-cottage-cheese-on-lettuce salad with a maraschino cherry on top. Gracious offers me milk but I insist on iced tea like she's having. There are sugar cookies for dessert.

And so we sit across the table from each other, she facing south, me north. I look to my right where the only dining room chair with armrests sits empty: Dad's head-of-the-family chair. On the left arm you can see where varnish was worn away years earlier by my father's watchband.

"Jeanine asked me about you maybe being a pallbearer at the funeral Monday, Larry, but I asked her not to—I just don't think you're quite ready for all that just yet . . . I don't think one should have to do that kind of special duty until he's eighteen—especially when there's an open coffin. There's plenty of time for all that later . . . I'm sure you'll be a pallbearer at other funerals . . . and then one day some of today's young boys who'll become townsmen may even provide you with that . . . oh, God . . ."

Her voice trails off, her eyes tear, and she brushes at them absently with the back of her hand. "Oh, *why* do I get these awful and despairing thoughts sometimes . . . they're not *me,* and they're not fit to be heard, I'm an optimist, but sometimes I just can't *help* it . . . he was *so* young! Just like Delbert!"

I reach across the table—Gracious has a clear plastic cover over an antique linen tablecloth—and give her hand a quick squeeze. "It's okay, Mamma . . . I really feel pretty awful about Andy too . . . it's really a crime he was taken so young."

Gracious leaves at 6:30, telling me to look for her to return around 9:30, then begins to sing softly a song they sing so loudly at church it makes the building shudder: "Love lifted me! . . . Love lifted me! When noth-ing else could help, Love lift-ted me . . ."

As soon as she's gone I look guiltily around the house, wander into the dining room and look at my reflection in Gracious's triangular corner cabinet where she keeps her best glassware and silver. Suddenly being alone is just a little exciting, even thrilling. I know I'll be seeing Deanna before too long, probably at the funeral Monday. I feel my blood speed up a bit. I recall evenings when Gracious would go out to school meetings during the war years and I would stare at my reflection in the cabinet's glass door, filled with fear: what if she has a car wreck? What if she dies—who's gonna take care of *me*?

I go sit on my bunk, run my hand up and down its valley, and regard the bouquet again: its medley of colors seems to penetrate my heart.

I look up at PALS, and absently turn on the old beehive Philco on my bedside table that Gracious used to listen to war news during the forties . . . in a minute or so it warms up and a jingle comes on:

"Robert Hall this season,
Will show you the reason,
Low overhead! Low overhead!"

I twist the dial and a song in progress comes on, one Anna sang on the last day of school in May when we walked home together:

"Glow little glow worm,
Glow and glimmer,
Swim through the sea of night
Little swimmer . . ."

On that day as we slow-walked along on the gravel road toward our homes, she was fiddling with some flowers as she often did; she seemed to have a special liking for blossoms of all kinds. She loved to make wreaths at Christmas, and to fashion tree ornaments from tin cans using tin snips. But most of those activities had to happen out of sight of her holy-roller parents, who were pillars of the Bi-Way Gospel Tabernacle, just out of town on the way to Skeegemog.

After "Glow Worm," Anna sang:

"Shrimp boats is a-comin'
Their sails are in sight
Shrimp boats is a-comin'
There's dancing tonight . . ."

Still restless, I slouch back into the dining room so I can again study my reflection in the glass door of the china cabinet: there I am, pretty much the same as a week ago, in my shorts and T-shirt, looking like I'm thinking hard about something. And in fact earlier I'd been thinking about Curly and Andy and had come to absolutely no conclusions at all. Except that Andy was dead and Curly was goofy in ways I could only guess at.

I wander back into my room thinking to thumb through my comics, though I don't read them much any more, except for *Classics,* and when I step from the living room into the sunroom, I see Anna sitting on the top step of my cement porch, her back to me, tearing petals from a daisy, letting them fall one at a time at her feet, and looking somberly off at the Chinese elms that rim our yard just before the road. She's wearing loose sky-blue shorts rather than the tight Levi's she favors, and a red T-shirt. Done with her daisy, she drops the stem and yellow center on the cement walkway and leans forward, resting her elbows on her knees, looking across at the vacant field where she and I and Alex and the Jenkins kids used to play softball on summer evenings when we were in grade school.

I realize we never will again.

I think over how to announce my presence, finally clear my throat and say, "Thanks a lot for the little bouquet, Anna, I really love the way Indian paintbrush and black-eyed Susans and daisies go together. I bet you could get a job in a flower shop. You'd be great at arranging."

She speaks without turning to look at me: "You're welcome. And welcome home. By the way, I don't 'spose you happen to know I turned fifteen yesterday?"

"No . . . no, I didn't, gosh, I'm sorry . . . happy birthday, Anna, gee, if I'd known I'd've gotten you a card and a present . . ."

"Well, maybe it's not too late yet."

"Well, sure thing. What would you like?"

"You," she says decisively, swiveling around on her bottom so she's facing me, lifting her head to look me full in the eyes. "I want you," she repeats, voice suddenly shaky, her eyes wide as if she can't believe what's coming from her lips. She commences to blush, and I pick it up somehow and feel my ears begin to burn.

"Well, gosh, Anna, you've got me already, gee, we been friends since even before kindergarten and you know how much . . . how much I like you . . ."

She rises from the porch, brushing dust or lint or whatever from her bottom and puts one Ked on the porch apron. Both French doors are drawn back so I reach out and pull back the screen door. "C'mon in, why don'tcha? Ma's off at choir practice in Deer Rapids, probably won't be back until 9:30 or so . . ."

She looks like she's thinking it over, then rises and crosses the porch. She brushes me slightly as she moves past, and one of her breasts slightly grazes my arm, making my breath catch and stick in my throat.

She sits on my bunk, her rear settling into the valley, leaning her back against the wall, then draws her legs up, crosses them, and fits the heels of her Keds under her bottom.

She looks at her bouquet in its slender pewter vase on my dresser but doesn't say anything.

She pats the mattress next to her.

This isn't the kind of thing where you waste a lot of time thinking, and I'm there in an instant, close to her, the lower part of my bare thigh touching hers. Her warmth makes air catch in my throat again.

"Oh, don't worry, Larry, I didn't really mean I wanted *you* for my birthday present," she says and gives a little sniff of what I guess you'd call disdain. "But a plain old kiss might be kinda nice."

I put my arm around her shoulder, but she doesn't turn into me, and I understand she wants me to pull her to me, or anyhow I hope that's true, because I pull on her shoulder and slowly turn her toward me until we're facing each other.

Slowly our faces move closer. Our lips meet. We press them together, don't do much else. My hand tightens slightly on her shoulder as if I'm afraid she may pull away. We look into each other's eyes: hers are big and blue and wide open, her eyebrows are copper and her nose freckled.

"Well, that was kinda nice, Larry, but now we're kinda stuck here in the middle, aren't we?" Deanna says and giggles. "Geeze. Y'know, if two people had to sleep on this thing they'd probably have to do it one on top of the other, like alligators . . ."

I overcome the swelling feeling in my throat enough to murmur, "Maybe that wouldn't be too bad if you liked the other person, and depending on if you got whichever you wanted, top or bottom."

"Which d'you think you are, Larry, a top or bottom person?"

How'd I get into this? Finally something squeezes itself through my throat: "I guess that'd depend on the other person . . ."

"Well, what if the other person was me?"

Deanna presses close, I can feel the cool tip of her nose against my throat. Out of my mouth come more words: "Well, I guess me on top, you on the bottom." Deanna giggles and snorts against my neck, dampening it, and we kind of tip over in the direction of the pillow and scrunch around until both of us are each lying facing each other, each half in the bunk's valley, our faces opposite each other's on the pillow.

Her lips are inches from mine, half-parted. "Do you like French kissing, Larry?"

"Uh, well . . ." But nothing else is willing to come out.

"Since we've never done it, except maybe sort of in your tent at Camp Greavey, maybe you don't really know how?"

"Uh, yeah, maybe . . ."

"It's really perfectly simple, you just keep breathing naturally and you bring your face toward mine and then you just sort of put your lips on mine, then we both sort of gently put out the tips of our tongues 'til they're between the lips of the other person and then our tongues touch and presto! We're French kissing . . . you can put your hand under my T-shirt if you want to, Larry."

I put my hand under her shirt and stroke her back, feeling the play of strong muscles, the warm smooth skin . . . which tells me also she's not wearing a bra. I'm surprised I hadn't noticed from looking at her. And then her mouth is on mine again and this time our tongues each go into the other's mouth and touch and swirl a bit until it's almost like they're playing a game.

Now her hand is up under my T-shirt, likewise stroking my back. And of course by now I have given up trying to stop the boner that has become painful and I keep trying to twist into a position that'll keep it away from Anna, but the goddamn valley keeps us close: every time I move a little away from Anna she rolls toward and into me and I'm sure she can feel it but she takes no notice and I don't know where the hell I am or really what I'm doing and I pretty much give up on thinking and pressing my mouth to hers again, seeking her tongue with my own.

"You can touch me in front now, if you want to, Larry."

I feel like I'm acting in a play; my arm of its own accord leaves her warm back, comes around to her front, drifts lightly over her bellybutton.

Impatiently she takes my wrist and moves my hand upward until it's covering her right breast. I feel a fleeting impulse to jerk my hand away, but my fingertips discover her nipple is not some little pip as I'd imagined but is about the size and shape of a new pencil's eraser and the kind of flange around is rougher than the smooth surrounding breast skin and my breath catches in my throat again.

Anna kisses my left ear, touching the lobe with her tongue.

And suddenly she is sitting up: with one brusque movement, she seizes the bottom of her T-shirt and pulls it over her head and tosses it on the floor, then lies back down and pulls me against her, pushing up my T-shirt at the same time so her nipples press into my bare chest and her warm breasts spread, adjusting to the shape of my chest.

Everything we do after that seems to come easily, wonderfully: her hand slipping down into the back of my shorts then coming around to the front, fiddling with the button, finally opening it. I want her to unzip me now but she doesn't. "Help me out of my shorts," she whispers. Since the top button is already undone, all I have to do is push the zipper down a few inches and start tugging at the bottoms and her shorts come loose easily and I slip them down over her thighs, my hand brushing over her slippery panties, and on past her feet and just about then she pulls my zipper down and shoves my shorts down to my knees, leaving my gleaming white Fruit of the Looms tenting out and I badly want her to touch me so when she doesn't I take her hand, put it on me and she squeezes and then for the first time I touch a woman between her legs, and I keep petting her, feeling her through the nylon, and that's when she—God, at last!—puts her hand into my skivvies and takes me, stiff and bare, into her hand and I put my hand inside her panties and for long—or maybe they're short—minutes we touch each other, lightly, lightly, caressing, and soon we're magically naked and are lying facing each other, the valley keeping us together, and I want the rest of it to happen but don't know exactly what to do or say or how to start.

"Please hand me my shorts, Larry . . ."

I do.

She takes something small out of a pocket, checks it herself, then holds it up for me to see. I recognize the round shape covered with red and white foil, the centurion's helmeted head: if you looked into the billfolds of most of the high school guys, you'd find a circle shape from just such a rubber beneath the leather.

"Honey, we have to be awfully . . . smart."

"Okay . . ."

At first I think she's thinking about her father Tyler Fuller coming to look for her. But from her look I see she means the rubber.

She tears the foil off and wads it up and puts it carefully into a pocket of her sky-blue shorts.

She extends the rubber to me on two fingers. I take it.

"You know how it works?"

"Uh, well, sort of . . . I guess sorta like this . . ."

"Yes, fit it over the top of your . . . your . . . no, you've got it wrong-side to there, Larry, turn it over the other way, yes, that's it, now just put it on and roll it all the way down . . . I don't need to find out whether or not sperms tickle . . . I know they like to swim . . ."

I do. As it rolls down, I watch myself bulging inside the milky white yet translucent rubber as it fits like skin around me and seems to melt. I roll it down to my pubic hair. The little tip is empty and folds over in an idiotic way that makes me want to laugh.

"Well," Deanna says, "I guess I'm ready if you are, well . . . maybe not quite, so why don't we just kind of sort of, um, well, touch each other a little more, does it really feel awfully awfully good to you, Larry, when I touch you like this?"

"Even better than that," I croak.

"Well, then, do you maybe think we oughta, um, really do . . . um, ah, do it, uh, make love, you know?"

"Suits me."

Nothing in previous fantasies and round-robin jacking off has prepared me for what is really, finally, the real thing: as I slip into Deanna and she tightens around me and gasps and I cry "God!" I know I've clearly entered some new and fantastic part of the world, learning in an eyeblink why everybody is always yearning and searching and yakking and singing about sex: because it's so far beyond good that you can't—I can't—properly even really begin to describe it.

"Oh my honey, oh, I think you just sort of *fainted,* maybe just for a second or two . . . I think fainting's sweet . . ."

She's cradling me against her, her nipple inches from my lips, her hand touching my forehead.

"Wow," I say, "I've . . . never . . . I don't know what to say . . ."

"I know," she says. "Me neither. But remember, my dear, we have to keep being *real* careful. Now see if you can roll that thing down now without spilling anything out of it and hide it someplace for now and later on *bury* it! Deep! Really, honey, we've just *got* to be careful, just really extra-extra careful with everything, Larry. And I mean everything."

"I know." I pick up the sticky rubber and hold it in my hand as I watch her pull her panties on, a beautiful movement, and then her shorts and T-shirt. It can't take her more than a few seconds.

It takes me a little longer because I'm still holding the rubber in my left hand, keeping the top of it pinched together. I'm still holding it as we sit side by side on the edge of the bunk. Finally I gingerly put it deep into the front pocket of my shorts.

"What'd you do, steal it from Alex?"

"Yes . . . well, no, actually, if you want to know the truth, I asked him and he gave it to me . . ."

"Alex *gave* it to you?"

She looks modestly down at her blue Keds on the floor near her feet. "Yes," she says, voice barely a whisper. "I asked him to get me one and he did. He's really a great brother. He'd never betray a secret. One of the reasons, just one, that I like you so much is that Alex likes you. A lot. He thinks that after Daddy dies, you and I'll get married and you and me and Alex will all live in the house and we'll all sit under the mulberry tree in the summer and laugh and drink beer."

"Wow. Well, who knows, maybe he's right."

"I don't know if we'll do this again, Larry—I hope so, that is if you really do love me, and I'm glad you were my first—but we do have to be *real* careful . . . oh God, don't let Daddy suspect anything, he'd kill me . . . really . . ."

"I wouldn't ever betray a secret either, Anna."

"I know, that's another reason why I chose you, apart from, well, because I kinda love you."

I feel the heavy weight of responsibility. To have someone other than my mother say she loves me scares me more than a little.

"Well, remember," Anna says, "when your next birthday rolls around, you've already had your present from me. Oh, no, I don't mean that—it wasn't any gift, Larry, maybe it was even you giving me my gift . . . you're so nice . . . and you know what you've done for me? You've made me a woman. And it was a very good experience too."

"Same here."

I look westward through the French windows at red glimmers of the fading sun. For some reason the word *woman* spoken aloud frightens me.

"I'll never forget," I say, inwardly shuddering at the inadequacy of words. But I have a lingering doubt I have to voice: "How'd you come to know about all this stuff, Anna?"

"Stuff?"

"Well, you know, about, well . . . I really like what you call it, making love . . . such pretty words . . ."

"Well, I learned stuff here and there, all us girls do, like from my older sister JannaMae, and from my older girlfriends, from reading and watching and listening and keeping an eye on how things work, Larry. And from Alex—he knows a real lot. And one thing and another. But I know what you're after. No, Larry, I haven't done what we did with anybody else. I thought a long time before I decided on you. You know how I've always liked you. So I guess now I can say I'm in love with you. Especially after, um, this evening. Can you say you love me—and no, I don't mean, can you say it, I mean, can you say it and *mean* it? Most any boy will tell most any girl whatever he thinks she might want to hear to get what he wants, which is to get into her pants—that's just the way things work. But you're not like that, that's another thing I like so much about you."

I don't think I've ever said "I love you" before, except maybe in the sort of nighttime ritual Gracious and I used to do up until I was seven. She'd come into the sunroom before I fell asleep and sit on the edge of my bunk and we'd sing what she called "our duet":

"How much do I love you?
I'll tell you no lie
How deep is the ocean?
How high is the sky?"

"I love you," I say.

Anna looks long and searchingly into my eyes. I think she's maybe going to ask me another question, but she puts a warm hand on the back of my neck and draws my face to hers.

Eleven

I'm in the tub when Gracious gets back around ten. Soapy water covers me to my chin as I stretch out in the tub. I'm concentrating on not getting a boner, but it's hard not to. I feel like I need water beyond this tub that I can twist and turn and writhe in.

A moment ago, a shaft of something had gone through me like an electric shock—I'd been examining a blood blister the size of a penny on my foreskin, wondering just how I'd gotten it, for I couldn't recall feeling any pinch or pain when Anna and I were together. Then I'd pushed my foreskin back for washing and beneath it had found a long spiraling coppery hair. I'd plucked it up and held it between thumb and forefinger, then lifted it toward the fluorescent light over the bathroom sink. Its reddish color deepened.

A shaft of pure fear had surged through me like electricity: how could it have gotten there with the rubber on?

It got stuck to me above the rubber and somehow . . .

When I pulled the rubber off, it somehow became attached to me . . .

Why, it was just floating along on a li'l ole breeze and happened to light on my dick . . .

That was when I heard our Chevy's tires crunching on the driveway gravel, then a few moments later Gracious opened the kitchen door, and I had guiltily dropped my hand in the soap water and the hair disappeared.

I follow Gracious's footsteps as she comes into the kitchen, passes through the dining room and into the living room. I hear her deposit a heavy object on her desk in the living room alcove between the two upright bookcases.

She must have gotten church out of her system, because she's humming "Sentimental Journey:" ". . . hmmm-hmm-hmm mm hmmm hm-hmm-mmm hmm-hmm," and when she begins to sing her voice is much lower than her hymn voice:

> ". . . *spent each dime I could afford,*
> *like a child in wild anticipation,*
> *I long to hear that 'All-aboard' . . ."*

The bathroom door's half-open and Gracious looks briefly in as she swings into her bedroom next door. "My," she calls to me, "I'll bet it feels good to get the dusk and dreck and sweat of the camp and the parade down the drain, Larry. There's nothing quite so calming as a good soak in a warm tub, is there?"

"How'd choir practice go?"

"Oh, it was wonderful, Larry, a kind of nice warm soak for the soul. The acoustics were absolutely perfect, such resonance, and did you notice the school tape recorder on my desk earlier? Well, I took it along and we were doing so well we recorded most of the session—I'll be going to bed soon, but it's on my desk, and if you'd like to play some of it, feel free—it certainly won't bother me or keep me awake. Maybe it would lull me. But oh my, I almost feel guilty for feeling better when I think of poor Andy . . . I just can't get that poor kid out of my mind, it's just *so* unfair . . ."

She's come to stand just outside the bathroom door.

I realize that Deanna and I had been so focused on each other since she came to my doorstep that we'd spared not a word nor even a thought for Andy whose funeral we'd both attend Monday in the Church of Christ, if Deanna's father, Tyler Fuller, a deacon of the Bi-Way Gospel Tabernacle on the way to Skeegemog, would let her go—who knew how holy rollers made decisions, but they sure ran a tight ship. I had a quick vision of Anna back in June on the first of the Friday night free shows put on by town merchants, where a projection booth—a tiny shanty on stilts—just off the gravel road that ran down to our house cast images on a white screen painted on the bricks of the north side of Guilder's General Store: about a dozen soberly dressed members of the Bi-Way Gospel Tabernacle's flock of four dozen had clustered around the booth, waiting for a Bugs Bunny cartoon to finish; then, just after "*Th-th-that's all, folks!*" and before the projectionist could get *They Drive by Night* up and running, the group began a hymn: "Near-er," they sang, "my God to Thee!"

> *"E'en though it be a cross*
> *That raiseth me;*
> *Still all my song shall be,*
> *Near-er, my God, to Thee . . ."*

Anna was sandwiched between her stocky sandy-haired deacon father and blimpish black-haired mother. She wore a high-collared long drab dress and her face was red as she fought to keep her bright eyes from looking up and around to see how many kids from school might be gawking at her.

> *"My rest a stone,*
> *Yet in my dreams I'll be*
> *Near-er, My God, to Thee . . ."*

It was a quick, successful operation: having gotten their hymn sung before the feature could start, the host, satisfied, left, crossing the main drag, then proceeding west on the road toward Skeegemog, where the Tabernacle waited just a few hundred yards away.

Anna's walk was jerky as they retreated, the first time I'd seen her less than graceful.

Gracious sighs. Having gotten no answer, she speaks: "I read some-where that the two great mysteries of life are love and death—I wonder if it's true?"

"Seems like there oughta be more to it than that."

"P'raps you're right—but if so, I wonder what those other as-pects and elements might be?" But I hear her going back to her room instead of waiting for an answer. Just as well, I don't have any, though the question lingers.

By the time I get into jeans and sweatshirt it's getting on toward 10:30. For some reason I'm tremendously hungry and so get out a quart of milk and take it and a bowl of Wheaties in on the dining room table. I study the cut glass sugar bowl on the table, and the sterling spoon that looks like a little scoop shovel. The style is Etrus-can, like the rest of our silver, Gracious has told me. I pour on more sugar than usual and have just begun eating when Gracious comes out in her blue bathrobe, looking tired but not unhappy.

"Well, Larry, did you do any more thinking?"

I look up. "Thinking?"

"Yes. You said there must be more great mysteries in life beyond just love and death. I just wondered if, after reflection, you decided that was really so, and if so, what you think those other mysteries might be. Honestly, I'd really like to know."

"Gosh, I don't know . . . guess I was just kinda talking off the top of my head without really thinking, Mamma . . . I guess love and death are good enough for me."

"I can think of yet another mystery, Larry—that mysterious sense of the sublime one sometimes gets that lets you know there are things beyond life's surface, like after I've swum . . . or when I'm standing in the Clearwater cemetery in the fall by Delbert's grave, even though I know he's not in it, and I look up at the lovely wood-ed hill rising beyond his grave where the leaves are all so brilliantly alive with such splendid colors. And too, I suppose one would have to consider sexuality an example of the sublime . . . though I some-times think it's something the gods oughtn't to have vouchsafed so lavishly to mere mortals . . ." She falters, as if she's just realized I'm really listening to her. "Oh, well, plenty of time for all of that later on, when you go off into the Great World as you must, Larry . . . I guess I was just joking, so pay me no mind . . ."

"Well, I don't plan going much of anywhere at the moment."

"Thankfully. Bless you. Goodnight, Larry. Sleep tight as a tick, as they say. And don't forget to brush your teeth."

"Goodnight, Mamma." She leaves for her bedroom and I take my bowl and spoon and wash, dry, and put them away.

Lying comfortably in the valley of my bunk, a sheet over my legs, I hear again, though just barely, those contending boats down at Silver Bridge powered by souped-up Mercury Lightning engines, their snarlings reduced by distance to a whiny but still urgent bee-buzz.

I think again of that single long spiraling reddish hair from Deanna that I'd lost when I heard Gracious coming into the house and had quickly dipped my hand in the bath water. And suddenly for no reason at all I'm hearing Curly's voice in my brain: "Hey, Larry, y'hear the one about the spastic whore? See, first one leg starts jumping around so they gotta hold'er down or she'll do damage to something—y'see it goes from one limb to another 'til they're all jitterbugging like crazy, and so they get these four huge whorehouse bouncers to hold her arms and legs down. So these guys are holding her down, see, one to a limb, and she's just a-spazzin' away, and the whoremaster comes in. He takes one look, hauls out his whang, goes over and crams it into her quivering snatch—yup, she's got the spaz there too—while these guys are just barely keeping her restrained, I tellya, pally, her legs and arms are just a-jumpin'. So the ole whoremaster winks at his bouncers, takes a deep breath, and says, 'Okay, guys . . . *turn 'er loose!*'"

Which leads me to wonder again if the vision Curly had created earlier of Andy's death was truth or bullshit—it didn't seem like it could be something in between, but then with Curly nothing was ever for sure: ambiguity, as he liked to say. I wonder if that same slim curved fleck of a moon now casting meager light on the yard was the last thing Andy ever saw. Besides the dark, of course.

I see Andy now, treading water, in just a little over his head, Curly, in up to his shoulders, relaxed, grinning, facing Andy, blocking him from swimming in, repelling him each time he tries to head for shore. No splashing, yelling, just some mild gasping, gulping, the silver bit of moon, and death. Or was all that a lie too—no, an *ambiguity*? And how will I ever know?

The answer is, I won't, any more than I'll ever know how my father died, at least exactly, and suddenly I am vivid and stiff, once again, with late-arriving rage: at *me!* Lamar-Larry!

I was never a match for a sharpie like Curly, who handled me as easily as if I were a child, suckering me into putting those marks on his neck, then threatening me, and then I was chickenshit when it most mattered, because I knew he'd follow through and I wasn't prepared to handle the losses involved. There was nothing useful I could have done for Andy, but I still feel damn lousy. I think of Camp G's garbage-devouring maggots, wonder if, after camp closes, they'll dwindle to a single ferocious victor, who then starves.

I lie back on my valleyed mattress, lace my fingers together, put my hands over the tanned skin between chest and belly, let my breathing slow down. This is how my hands will be arranged after I die, unless I happen to be burned to a crisp or blown to bits.

I shut my eyes, bring a hand to my face. My fingers are cool and soothing as I rub the bridge of my nose that Anna'd kissed less than—what? Almost—only!—two hours ago? I think I can still smell her on my fingertips through the scent of Lifebuoy. I keep my eyes closed, deciding I'll rest a few minutes before trying to figure out what the next thing will be. I still find it hard to believe that I have touched and kissed and been with Anna in ways Gracious would surely call "intimate." I'll never be the same again, and I'm glad. I want my lips on Anna's, on her breasts, again and again, I want to kiss her so deeply it takes her breath away. Shit—I've given myself a boner. I think I feel a little ache where the blood blister is.

I turn on the old Philco, and as it warms up, I can still hear, faintly, those snarling outboard engines two miles away and I imagine the light racing craft shooting down Silver River, then under the swing bridge, then gaining the full body of Silverfish Lake, and how wide the lake before them would look.

The radio awakens with Frank Sinatra singing, "When somebody loves you, it's no good unless he loves you . . . all the way . . ."

I get up, switch off the radio, pull on my jeans and sweatshirt, go to the open French doors, pull back the screen door, and go barefoot out into the yard. The damp grass feels great on my soles.

Pale light flickers as dark clouds pass over the moon's half-vertical grin.

Why can't I get Curly out of my head—it's as if the bastard's bored his way into my brain the way some say earwigs do, and every thought I have seems to bear the black edge of his influence; even now I can hear him: "Hey, Larry, y'hear 'bout the guy trying to swear off pounding his pud? He'd put his hand around his dick, and whenever he starts to get a boner he squeezes it and says, '*Die! Die! Die!*' Works pretty well, but then after a while he starts to get sloppy and it goes like this: 'Die! Die! Di-die Di-die die-die-die . . .'"

I think of knot-fancier and -practitioner Ed Gentry and his admiration, no, love, for knots' function and beauty, and his point that if the rope's sound and execution proper, a good knot'll never let you down. It feels damn good to have at least one thing immune from Curly's notions of ambiguity.

I hear sounds from the living room—Gracious must have come out and turned on our 17-inch Arvin TV to catch the eleven o'clock news.

Guessing she won't bother checking up on me, I stay where I am, staring through the limbs of the Chinese elms at the white scrap of moon. I suddenly realize I still have that used rubber in the front pocket of my shorts. I'd planned on burying it in our vacant lot that my parents got years ago so nobody could build on it and mess up their sunsets.

Well, I won't forget it this time and will bury it pronto.

So where will we all be, me, Curly, Anna, Alex, Gracious, ten years from now? Twenty? Thirty? A kind of vision comes to me, what Alex foresaw: Anna and Alex and I are in our twenties, we three have taken over the Fuller house after Tyler dies, Anna and I are married, Alex is still my best friend . . . maybe Alex will be married or have a girlfriend, and I'll never see nor hear from or about Curly again . . . but this fantasy turns to froth when I hear a sound behind me; before I can fully turn, Gracious has come through the sunroom doors, down the steps, and is beside me in her blue bathrobe, gazing like me through the branches of the Chinese elms at the moon. Black clouds are drifting off into the northwestern sky. My mother puts an arm around my shoulders. I freeze for a second, thinking of that rubber in my pocket.

"I wanted to get the weather for tomorrow on TV, Larry . . . looks like it's going to be pretty much like today's and . . . oh, how I hate to tell you this, but—Mister Gibb? Perkins Gibb? Your camp director? I just heard it on the news. He's dead, Larry, he died earlier this evening . . . it was said he may have died of a massive heart attack due to a congenital heart defect . . . oh I *thought* he looked awfully tired at the parade today."

I have to say something. "Yeah, he did look kinda gray . . . gosh, he was a nice man . . . way too good for that outfit . . ."

"The camp?" she says in astonishment. "Too good for a Boy Scout Camp? Why, what*ever* do you mean by that, Larry?"

"I don't know, I guess I'm just so surprised I don't know what to say . . . forget it. He was kind of hard to understand sometimes, but you for sure knew his heart was in the right place."

She doesn't press me further. "Well, I'm sorry to have been the bearer of such sad tidings, Lamar . . . it's certainly a good thing to feel sad about both Andy and Mr. Gibb, but please don't dwell too much on them for now. We've the funeral Monday, of course. Well, try to get a good night's sleep. Good night. Again."

Before she reaches the porch, I hear her say in her book-quoting voice, " 'Now thou have come into a feast of death.' "

The line makes me shudder. Well, I won't think of the dead. I don't want to. I want to think of Deanna in new jeans, sitting in a washtub full of warm water so that when she takes them off they'll dry in the shape of her bottom. And I want to think of her breasts and nipples . . . and oh Christ, I've given myself a boner again, and am struck by a longing for Deanna so intense I feel lightheaded, as if I might faint. Again. Well, at least it doesn't seem likely I'll turn queer overnight. And anyhow I've now seen a grown man blow a fart in public and get away with it. And I didn't after all have to fill out that "extensive" questionnaire Perky'd threatened us with on the first day of Camp G. I know now why the bowline is "king of knots." And I think Curly's basically right with all that junk about ambiguity. Also I've got an 1820 U.S. penny—and don't worry, Curly, I won't mess it up by polishing or cleaning. And I know there's probably nothing that's truly indivisible.

I go back to the porch and sit down again upon the top step, hands out on either side like outriggers.

The sun's warmth has by now pretty much left the concrete, but I move my toes around and find a faintly warm spot.

I think of the way Deanna says catsup, as if it were two distinct but related words, never "ketchup" like the rest of us: "Cat-sup," I say. "Cat-sup. Cat-sup."

I long to hear her say it again, remember suddenly that I told her I loved her, feel a pang of fear.

A shooting star streaks across the western sky but its bright finger of white light is extinguished before I can properly register it. I forgot to make a wish. Probably just as well, I wouldn't have known what to ask for anyhow, beyond hoping that things will turn out okay for most everyone.

I remember Perky's deep somber voice as he sang, "Gone are the days, when my heart was young and gay . . ."

And I remember Anna and me walking home together on the last day of school in May, both of us ready for summer's promise, me wanting to reach out and take her hand, she singing, "Shrimp boats is a-comin' . . . there's dancin' tonight . . . why don'tcha hurry hurry home . . . why don'tcha hurry hurry home . . ."

Biographical Note

Geoffrey Clark was born and raised in lower northern Michigan. He is a graduate of the Iowa Writers' Workshop and is author of eight works of fiction, among them *Schooling the Spirit, Jackdog Summer, Wedding in October,* and *Necessary Deaths.* He retired as Professor of Creative Writing at Roger Williams University in 1999. He lives in Warren, Rhode Island.